Ansley has been looking for his dragon since Byron was taken from him a hundred years ago. The sacrifice of his shield and the man he was in love with was necessary, but Ansley can't find peace, and neither can the other five mages he considers his brothers, who also shared that sacrifice. They've been without their other half for so long that some of them have lost hope.

But not Ansley.

Parker has no memory beyond the past hundred years. He's been moving every ten years or so because he's not aging — which probably has to do with his ability to shift into a dragon — but this time around, it's harder to leave everything behind. He doesn't have a choice, though.

When Ansley finally finds the right spell, it leads him straight to Byron. But Byron isn't Byron anymore. A hundred years and no memories turned him into a new man.

A man Ansley likes even more than he did Byron.

Ansley's job is to find the other five dragons, but with the threat that caused the mages to lose the dragons rising again, he might not be able to do it in time.

And if he can't, it could mean death for all of them.

Sky High
Copyright © 2023 Catherine Lievens
ISBN: 978-1-4874-3832-6
Cover art by Angela Waters

Published by eXtasy Books Inc

Look for us online at:
www.eXtasybooks.com

Sky High
Mages & Dragons 1

By

Catherine Lievens

CHAPTER ONE

Seeking spells. They hadn't been Ansley's specialty until he and the other mages had lost their dragons. Since then, he'd cast hundreds of them, if not more, and not one had worked. What did he have to do to get his dragon back? To bring the dragons back to all the mages?

That was what Ansley had been obsessing over for decades. He'd started with the simplest spells when he and the others were still healing from the fight with Carlyle, and when those hadn't worked, he'd moved on to more complicated spells. By now, he'd reached the point where he was modifying the spells to give himself hope that one day, he'd find the dragons.

Yesterday had not been that day. He wasn't sure about today yet, but he'd try.

He always did.

"You could get your head out of your books at least during the meals," Jarvis teased from the other side of the table.

Ansley blinked up at him. "What?" He'd heard Jarvis, but his brain was having a hard time making sense of the words. He was always like this when he was deep in thought, especially when thinking about spells, which was pretty much always these days.

Jarvis's smile was indulgent. "Never mind. What has you so focused this morning?"

Penley snorted. "What do you think? There's only ever one thing on his mind."

Jarvis arched a brow. "Maybe, but he's only doing it for all of us."

"I didn't say it was a bad thing. I want my shield back as much as you do."

They all did. Even though they didn't need their shields anymore, what with Carlyle being trapped, they didn't feel complete without their dragons. It made them vulnerable and exposed them to other mages and danger, and it had been that way for so long that Ansley had lost count of the years. He didn't want to think about how long he'd been without Byron. He just wanted Byron back.

He got to his feet, not hungry anymore. Penley had reminded him he had work to do, and the sooner he started, the sooner he'd find the right spell.

"You should eat," Jarvis said.

"I did."

Jarvis looked down at Ansley's plate. "You should eat more. It won't do anyone any good if you faint during a spell."

"I'm not going to faint."

Even though Ansley routinely forgot to eat. His entire focus had been on his spells and finding the dragons for so long that more often than not, he barely thought about anything else. He was lucky he had his brothers and the others who shared the castle with them. If it weren't for them, he would have become a hermit who never left his rooms. As it was, the only reason he did leave them was that, like Jarvis had said, he needed food.

Jarvis sighed. "Not today, but eventually, this will catch up to you. Do you really think Byron would want you to work yourself to the bone to find him?"

A flash of pain threatened to break Ansley's heart. "I don't know what Byron would want," he snapped.

"I'm sorry. I'm not trying to get you to stop, just to take care of yourself. We don't want to lose you. We've already lost too much."

Ansley looked around the table. Not everyone was there, but the ones who were present nodded at Jarvis's words. It touched Ansley, but it wasn't enough.

It never would be until they found their dragons.

Every mage had a shield. It had always been that way, and it always would be. The shields were dragon shifters who protected mages during battles and while they were casting spells. Both in battle and in spell casting, mages had to focus on what they were doing, which exposed them to whoever wanted to attack. That was where the dragons came in.

Or rather, it had been.

Most mages still had their dragons. It was just Ansley and his brothers who didn't.

He swallowed and grabbed his notebook from the table. "I have work to do," he repeated.

This time, no one tried to stop him. They knew it was useless, and he was both relieved and grateful. He shouldered a massive responsibility—finding the dragons. His brothers could do the same spells he did, but they hadn't been working on them for as long as he had. Every one of them had their specialty, and spells of the seeking kind were Ansley's.

Yet he couldn't find the dragons.

Ansley quickly left the dining room. His footsteps echoed against the stone in the hallway, giving him the impression of an empty space.

Like his heart.

He didn't fool himself. Finding the dragons would be hard, if not impossible. They all wondered why their dragons hadn't found them in so many years, and while they couldn't know for sure what Carlyle had done in his last spell, it had to have been bad. It had made the dragons stay away, something they wouldn't have done if they hadn't been forced to.

Well, most of them wouldn't have. Ansley couldn't be sure

about Byron because they hadn't been that close, even though they'd shared the bond every mage and their shield shared. The thought of Byron staying away from him on purpose hurt.

He needed to have more faith. Byron hadn't known about Ansley's feelings for him, but that didn't mean he would have stayed away. Like all dragons, he understood how vital his role was when it came to protecting the mages. He'd have been here, doing exactly that, if he'd been able to.

Which meant he wasn't.

Ansley and the other mages had obsessed over why the dragons were staying away for decades, and none of them had an answer. Ansley knew that a few of them had started to wonder if maybe their dragons were dead, but Ansley didn't feel that was so. Maybe that was just because he wanted to keep hoping, or maybe he was right. Whatever the case, eventually, he'd find the dragons.

The problem was that he didn't know what state they'd be in when he did.

He'd been playing with yet another seeking spell lately, but it hadn't worked so far. He'd woken up this morning thinking about another tweak he could make while casting it, though, and he was eager to try. The hope to find the dragons had dimmed over the years, but it was always fun for him to play with magic. He learned a lot, which meant that even if they never found the dragons, he'd have benefited from all of this.

But he'd much rather have the dragons.

He turned the corner and slammed against a hard chest. Two hands grabbed his arms, keeping him on his feet, and he blinked up at another one of his brothers. Keylon hadn't been at breakfast, but he was headed toward the dining room.

"You have to stop daydreaming before you fall down the stairs or some shit like that," Keylon said, releasing Ansley.

Ansley rubbed the back of his neck. "I'm sorry. I was

thinking about—"

"A seeking spell," Keylon finished the sentence.

Ansley glared at his brother, but there was no heat behind it.

He and Keylon weren't related by blood. Ansley wasn't related by blood to anyone at this point, because his family had died long ago. It didn't mean he was alone. He and the other mages he lived with had been together since before the spell that had torn their shields away from them, and they'd grown even closer since then. They were brothers, even though there was no shared blood between them. There didn't need to be.

"I thought of another tweak I can make that should work," Ansley told Keylon.

Keylon didn't look excited, which Ansley understood. The only reason Ansley was still doing this was that he didn't know what he'd do if he gave up.

"Sometimes, I wonder if it's worth it," Keylon murmured.

"If what is worth it?"

Keylon gestured at Ansley. "You haven't been yourself since the dragons were taken from us. I don't like seeing how much you overwork yourself, and I'm not the only one. We need you to be healthy, and I'm not sure you are."

Ansley bristled. "What would you want me to do? Give up? Do you think I can't find them?"

Keylon hesitated. "We don't even know if they're alive."

It hurt to hear those words, especially because it was something Ansley wondered every time he cast a seeking spell. Why couldn't he find the dragons? Why hadn't they found the mages?

He straightened his back. "I don't know if they're still alive, but if they are, I'll find them, even if it kills me."

"That's what I'm afraid of," Keylon said. There was real fear in his voice.

The loud music made the floor vibrate under Parker's shoes. He was used to it and hummed along to the rhythm as he filled a glass with beer. He placed the glass onto the counter, sliding it toward the man who'd ordered it. The man nodded and took the glass, stepping away from the counter and freeing a spot there.

From behind the bar, Parker saw the door open. The place was fairly busy, which was good, but he was exhausted and couldn't wait for this night to be over. He wanted nothing more than to go home, shower, and get into bed.

Matthias walked in.

Parker grinned even though Matthias wasn't a client. Matthias looked up, grinned back, and waved, and Parker got his best friend's favorite drink ready.

Every movement Parker made was familiar. And not for the first time, the thought of leaving all of it behind made his chest ache. He didn't want to go. This place had been his home for almost a decade by now, though, and it was time for him to move on. If he didn't, someone would end up noticing he wasn't aging, and he'd be in trouble.

If only he could remember what had happened to him, maybe he'd be able to find where he belonged.

He shook himself. He had things to focus on, and his fucked-up memory wasn't one of them. Who cared if he didn't remember who he was? He didn't need to remember. He just had to be here, do his job, and earn money. He'd need it when he moved.

And he would have to soon.

It wasn't something he could avoid. People tended to notice when he didn't age, and he'd already stuck around this small town for too long. The only reason he had was Matthias, and he was surprised his best friend hadn't noticed anything weird about him in the years they'd been friends. He would eventually, and Parker wouldn't know what to tell him when he did.

Yeah, I'm not aging, and by the way, I can turn into a massive fucking dragon, but I'm still your best friend, right?

Parker snorted. He had no idea how Matthias would react if he said something like that, but he wanted to believe it would be good. Matthias loved romance and fantasy novels and movies, and he'd be excited to have his own dragon shifter.

Maybe.

Or maybe he'd freak out and run away screaming, and Parker would have to leave in a rush. He didn't want to think of a world in which Matthias hated him or was afraid of him, which was why he'd never told Matthias about himself. He never would, either. The thought of leaving Matthias behind without explaining what was happening hurt, but Parker wasn't sure there was any way around it.

Matthias finally reached the bar and beamed when Parker placed a glass in front of him.

"Love you," he said, grabbing it and taking a sip.

Parker rolled his eyes, pushing the pain and confusion away for a bit. "You only love me for my bartender skills."

"Why else would I?" Matthias asked with a wink. He leaned against the counter and looked around. "It's hopping tonight. I bet you're exhausted."

"I am, but it's good to have so much business, so I'm not going to complain."

"Oh, you *are*. It's going to be all *my back hurts, my feet hurt, and I'm tired.*" Matthias hunched his shoulders and tried to sound like Parker.

Parker scowled at him—he didn't sound like an old man, dammit.

"You're getting old," Matthias declared.

Parker sucked in a breath. He *wasn't* getting old, which was the problem. Still, he plastered a smile on his face, not wanting Matthias to realize that what he'd said hurt in a way it shouldn't. "We can't all be as young as you."

"We're about the same age," Mattias pointed out.

If only he knew.

Parker swallowed. He'd been thinking about ghosting Mattias, leaving without telling his best friend anything, but he couldn't do that to him. He couldn't tell him the truth, but the least he could do was explain he was planning on selling the bar. Matthias would be horrified and then angry, especially when Parker couldn't give him an explanation he could believe. Wanting to see a different part of the country wouldn't be enough, and even if it was, he'd insist on coming along. That was why Parker was tempted to just leave. If he did, Matthias wouldn't be able to follow, which was kind of the point.

Parker didn't know what any of this meant. He didn't know if his immortality and the fact that he didn't age were linked to his being able to turn into a dragon.

That was how he'd woken up a long time ago. The first thing he remembered was opening his eyes to see he was on the ground in a forest. He had no idea how he'd gotten there, but he'd been in his dragon form. He'd shifted back quickly. It had felt natural, as if it was something he was used to doing, but he'd known that most of the world around him was human. He'd always hidden that he was a dragon shifter, and he always would.

The problem was that when he'd awakened, he hadn't known anything about himself. He remembered the world was human and that he needed to hide his dragon and most of the things normal people would remember, but nothing about himself or his life. He didn't know if he had a family. He didn't know how he'd ended up in the forest.

He didn't even know his name.

For a while, he'd changed his name every time he moved.

It had felt like a new start every time, and he'd needed that, but he'd grown tired of it. He didn't want to continue moving. He wanted to settle down, maybe find someone he could share his life with.

As if he could ever have that.

He was lucky he'd found a best friend this time around. Usually, he tried keeping people away because it hurt too much to lose them when he had to move on, but Matthias hadn't taken no for an answer. He'd pushed his way into Parker's life until he'd become part of it, and he'd made Parker's days and nights less lonely. Parker didn't want to go back to being alone, or to leave Matthias behind.

But he would have to.

He swallowed and looked around. Everyone had a drink, which meant he had a few moments to talk to Matthias. He leaned forward, his heart in his throat, words on his lips. "Mattie?"

Matthias twisted to look at Parker. "Yeah?"

"I need to tell you something."

Matthias turned around to face Parker. "You don't look good. Are you getting sick? I can take over the bar if you want to go home."

The door opened again, getting both their attention. A woman came in, and Parker knew the moment was over.

"Hey, it's Jasmine," Matthias said, pointing at his sister. "Maybe she could take over for a while, and I can take you home."

Parker forced himself to smile. "I'm fine."

"Are you sure? You look a little pale."

"Like you said before, I'm tired and getting old. That's all."

Matthias stared for a moment. Parker had no doubt his best friend knew he was lying, but thankfully, Matthias didn't say anything about it. Parker would have broken down into tiny pieces if he had.

Instead of letting the heartbreak get to him, he focused on work. It was the safest thing for him to do right now, but unfortunately, it didn't solve his main problem.

Should he ghost Matthias and hurt him in a way Matthias might never recover from, or should he tell him he was leaving and deal with the outcome of that?

"Where do you need this?" Etta asked. She raised the candle she was holding so Ansley could see what she was talking about.

He peered down at his notes. "At the top of the circle," he directed.

She nodded and set the candle down, then took a step back. She wasn't a mage, just a human, but she knew the truth about Ansley and the other mages. They trusted her, which was one of the reasons she'd become Ansley's personal assistant.

The main reason was that she was awesome.

"What now?" she asked, putting her hands on her hips as she turned to look at him.

He peered at the circle he'd drawn on the floor of his office. They'd gathered all the ingredients for the spell, including the things Ansley had wanted to tweak. The only thing left to do was for him to cast the spell, and like always, he was nervous.

What if it didn't work? What if it did work?

He swallowed.

"Step to the side, like always," he told Etta.

She didn't hesitate to obey his order. She flattened her back against the wall and gathered her skirt around her legs. She looked excited, but she always was when Ansley did magic. She didn't even care if it didn't work. She just liked watching him do it, and Ansley had stopped trying to convince her to step out of the room a while ago. The spell he was casting wouldn't be a danger for her, anyway.

He carefully stepped into the center of the circle, taking his notebook with him. He looked around one last time, checking that everything was where it should be. Etta had lit the candles, and the air smelled heavily of herbs. They were soothing, and Ansley focused on the scent rather than on what he was about to do.

He clutched his notebook to his chest and closed his eyes. The room was warm, with the fire going in the fireplace. That was where Etta had dropped the herbs that were burning and scenting the air, a careful mix that would help Ansley focus on the spell. There were other elements to the spell, gemstones and different kinds of wood which he hoped would make a difference. He could feel their energy pressing against him, pushing him and giving him support.

Magic was everywhere around him—in the air, the water, the stone of the walls and floor. Ansley and the other mages could use that magic to do things, and in theory, they could do so without needing the candles and everything else. That was the case when it came to small spells, but for bigger things, Ansley needed to feel he was working with something physical, which was why he'd insisted on the stones and the herbs and whatnot. Eventually, the right combination of things would lead him to the dragons, or at least, he hoped so. He just needed to find the right way to cast the spell, the right wording to ask the magic to find his dragon.

He took a deep breath, then another, and focused on Byron. He was somewhere out there, living his life, and Ansley wondered what that life was like. Hopefully, he'd find out soon.

He regulated his breathing until it was nice and slow and the room was almost entirely silent. Etta was still there, but she'd learned how to behave when he cast a spell, and she knew not to distract him.

She was the best assistant Ansley had ever had.

Once he felt ready, he squared his shoulders. He reached out for the magic with his mind, smiling when it answered his touch. Keeping as much focus as he could, he gathered the magic and directed it to the map he'd placed at the center of the circle, right in front of him. The dragons could be anywhere, but he'd already decided to start with the country they were in. The US was big enough that it would hopefully contain at least a few of the dragons, if not more. Once he got the spell right, he could expand the search to other countries if necessary.

Ansley focused the magic on thoughts of Byron. He remembered him as a human, even though it was getting harder and harder as time passed. Byron had been thirty-two when he'd vanished from Ansley's life, and they'd only found each other a year prior to that. He wasn't that much taller than Ansley, but instead of being slim, he was well-built, with broad shoulders and powerful arms that yielded a sword as if it were easy. Ansley had never known how to behave when Byron stared at him with his brown eyes, and he'd been too afraid to ask him for his thoughts.

And Byron's dragon. He was a brilliant copper color in that form, like metal. Ansley had ridden him many times, and he remembered well the feeling of having so much power under him. He'd started falling in love with Byron the first time they'd met, but he'd fallen deeper the first time Byron had allowed him to ride his dragon form.

They'd still been trying to find a way to work together when Byron had been taken from Ansley, and Ansley wanted that opportunity back.

He wanted Byron back.

With Byron's image in his mind, he molded the magic into an arrow. Then he threw it forward in the direction of the map. It would be easier for him to do this with his eyes open, but he was afraid he'd lose his focus if he did that. He could try again later if it didn't work this time.

Ansley didn't know what would happen, but he knew what he expected. No matter how much he wanted the spells to work, they never did, and when he opened his eyes, he fully expected the same to have happened this time around. Instead, he heard Etta suck in a breath and quickly turned his attention to her.

"What is it?" he asked.

She pointed her finger toward him, or rather, toward the center of the circle. When Ansley looked down, he understood why.

The map was still smoking. He hadn't seen the fire, but there was no ignoring the burned spot on the map. Ansley dropped to his knees, reaching for the map but afraid to touch it. The burned spot wouldn't disappear if he did, but it felt like it would.

He touched the corner of the map and leaned forward. "Pennsylvania," he whispered.

Etta moved toward him, freezing when she reached the circle. She knew better than to step in when he was using magic, but the magic was gone now. It was peaceful again, resting after being used, and Ansley waved at Etta to join him.

She dropped to her knees, too, and together, then looked down at the map.

"Which one is it?" she asked. "Yours?"

Ansley's mouth was dry. "You think we found him?"

"Isn't that what the burned spot means? You did that on purpose, right?"

Ansley nodded curtly. "I did. This was how the spell was supposed to work."

"Then it looks like it worked. Were you thinking about Byron?"

Ansley looked away. He didn't have to answer for Etta to know she was right. Maybe he should have started with one of the other dragons, but he was selfish. He wanted the first dragon they found to be his.

"So Byron's in Pennsylvania," Etta said.

Panic seized Ansley's chest. "Shit." He dropped on his ass. "I did it."

Etta beamed. "You did. You found Byron, and he's in the country."

Not that it mattered. Jarvis's specialty was portals, and Ansley had no doubt he'd take him anywhere on the planet if it meant finding the dragons.

Byron was alive. The spell had worked. Ansley had found his shield, but he still didn't know one thing.

Why hadn't the dragons come to them? Why had they all stayed away instead of reuniting with their mages? Byron might not have wanted to come back, but what about the others?

The question Ansley had avoided asking himself was unavoidable now.

What if all the dragons had wanted to stay away from the mages?

CHAPTER TWO

"Maybe we should wait," Ansley said.

Jarvis looked at him like he was nuts. To be honest, Ansley felt a bit out of sorts. He'd been working toward this for decades. He'd been trying to find a way to get Byron back, and that was the only thing he'd focused on for so long that he didn't know what life was like without that goal in mind.

And now that he'd found Byron, he wanted to wait?

But Jarvis didn't understand. He and his dragon, Marlow, had been together for a long time. They'd been like an old married couple, even though they'd never tied the knot. Jarvis had faith in Marlow, and now that they were one step closer to finding the dragons, he couldn't wait to get his man back. Ansley understood, but the relationship he'd had with Byron had been very different.

Ansley was pretty sure that Byron had viewed him as an annoying younger brother, even though he hadn't been that much younger. He'd kept Ansley around because he had to and it was his duty, but he'd never seemed very interested in him. On the other hand, Ansley had fallen madly in love with him, and sometimes, he wondered if Byron had known and that was why he'd stayed away after he and the others had disappeared. Maybe he'd wanted a chance to escape Ansley. Maybe he hadn't wished to be Ansley's dragon anymore.

The problem was that mages and dragons didn't choose each other. The magic did that for them. In this case, it had decided that Ansley and Byron belonged together. Neither of them had been able to refute that, even though Byron had no doubt been tempted.

So the truth was that Ansley was anxious. What if he found Byron but Byron didn't want him to? What if Byron had been hiding because he didn't want anything to do with him? Ansley wasn't sure he could stand the kind of pain that would come with that knowledge. He was also afraid of other things, like what if Byron had been dead all this time? Ansley had found him, but he had no way of knowing what state Byron was in.

Jarvis grabbed Ansley's shoulder and squeezed. It helped ground Ansley, but not enough to get rid of the fear.

"I know you're scared," Jarvis murmured. "I am, too, and Byron isn't even my dragon. After so many years of working on this, we finally see an end. We're about to find the truth, and our world will drastically change once we do. We'll finally know what happened to the dragons, and I realize it might not be good. We can't hide from this, though. We need to know if our dragons are alive."

Even though Ansley had the same fear, he told himself to trust his instinct and the magic. "I know they are. Don't you?"

Jarvis smiled. "I feel that Marlow is alive, but I've been wrong before."

"*You* might have been, but not the magic. If it's telling you Marlow is alive, then he is."

"Shouldn't the same go for Byron?"

"He's alive." Ansley was sure of that. He couldn't listen to the fear that his dragon could have died. It wasn't the magic talking. It was the part of himself that believed he wasn't good enough and never would be.

"Then let's go find your dragon. Maybe we'll finally find out why they haven't come to us."

It would be a relief, but it didn't help Ansley feel any less terrified. Still, he didn't have a choice. He'd found Byron, and Jarvis and the other mages expected him to get his dragon back. They wanted answers, and having found Byron gave them hope they'd find their own dragon soon.

Ansley wouldn't disappoint them.

He nodded, and Jarvis took his hand away. He raised it and murmured a few words, and a portal appeared in front of them.

It was like a window to another part of the world. Ansley could open portals if he needed to, but it was nowhere near as elegant as when Jarvis did it. Jarvis hadn't even had to close his eyes to focus, for fuck's sake. He was also extremely precise, while Ansley had been known to end up in a different part of town from where he'd tried to go.

Even in a different country once. But Ansley didn't talk about that.

After finding out where Byron was, Ansley had run to the other mages, and they'd started planning. Ansley had cast the spell again, this time with a map of Pennsylvania, and then once they had the name of the town, they'd printed a map of the place from the Internet. Ansley had pinpointed Byron's position, which meant he and Jarvis knew where they were going. They'd used the Internet to explore the area around the spot where Byron was supposed to be, and Jarvis had found a good place to open the portal. No one would see them, which mattered, because they didn't want humans to find out magic was real and all that stuff.

That was why the portal had opened onto a wooded area. When Ansley and Jarvis stepped through, Ansley couldn't see anything but trees, but he could hear the sound of cars nearby. He knew they were behind the bar where apparently Byron spent a lot of his time.

Ansley's heart stuttered.

Jarvis looked around, then closed the portal. He knew where they were going as well as Ansley, but he didn't move and waited for Ansley to make the first move. They were about to find Byron, Ansley's dragon, not Jarvis's. Ansley knew Jarvis would let Ansley do this the way he felt was better.

The problem was that Ansley had no idea what he was doing. He had no idea what would happen once he found Byron, and he was afraid of finding out.

"Let's go," he said, even though he wanted to run home.

He started walking, but Jarvis grabbed his shoulder and turned him in the right direction. He didn't even tease Ansley this time, but Ansley was angry at himself. His dragon was so close that he could feel the magic vibrating around him, yet he couldn't find the right direction? It was no surprise that Byron had wanted nothing to do with him when they'd first found each other. Ansley was as much of a disaster now as he had been back then.

He and Jarvis walked between the trees until they reached the edge of the wooded area. They stepped into a parking lot behind the bar the spell had indicated. It was the middle of the day, so the lot was almost empty. Two cars were there, though, and Ansley knew that one of them had to belong to Byron.

"We should probably wait until the bar opens tonight," he said.

Jarvis shook his head. "We shouldn't. We don't know how Byron will react to seeing you, so it's best to do this during the day when the bar is closed."

He was right.

Since there was no going back, Ansley moved forward. He walked through the parking lot, then around the bar until he got to the entrance. The door was closed, but he still reached for it, pausing just before his palm could hit the wood.

Byron was behind this door. Ansley could feel it. He had no idea how Byron would react to his presence, but he was here now. No matter how much it hurt or scared him, he needed to find out.

He pressed his hand against the door and pushed it open.

It was time to tell Matthias. That was why Parker had asked him to come to the bar this morning, when he wouldn't have an excuse not to tell his best friend he was leaving. No one would interrupt them, and Matthias would have the privacy to rant and yell the way Parker had no doubt he would need to. Matthias would be heartbroken and angry, and Parker wouldn't blame him.

He felt the same way.

He didn't want to leave, but he couldn't explain that. He couldn't explain to his best friend that he seemed to be immortal and that while Matthias would grow old, Parker never would. Even if he tried to tell Matthias that, he had no doubt his friend would laugh in his face. He wouldn't believe him, and Parker couldn't blame him. He wouldn't believe it himself if he wasn't living it.

But he *was* living it, and he hadn't aged since he'd woken up a hundred years ago. He didn't know why or how it worked, and he didn't know if it would ever change. It hadn't until now, which meant he was losing yet another home and the few people he could call family.

"Okay, spill it," Matthias suddenly said, putting down the glass he'd been drying.

Parker blinked up at him. He'd been cleaning the counter, but he hadn't moved from his spot in a few minutes, and the wood shone under his rag. It was no surprise that Matthias knew something was up or that he was asking for an explanation. He'd never been one to hide from complications, which was something Parker had always admired.

Parker set down the rag. He didn't know where to start, and he looked around, his heart aching at the thought he'd have to sell the place.

"You're starting to worry me," Matthias said, stepping closer and putting a hand on Parker's arm. "You wanted time with me, but I can see something's on your mind. What is it?"

"I have something to tell you," Parker managed to get out.

For some reason, Matthias's expression turned fearful. "I knew it," he whispered. "What is it? Please tell me you're not ill."

Parker jerked away. "Of course not. Why would you think that?"

Matthias glared. "Why wouldn't I? You've been acting like someone killed your puppy for the past few days. I've given you time and space, but you still haven't talked to me, and I've been worried. Now, you say you need to talk to me, and something is clearly wrong. If you're not sick, what is it?"

Parker swallowed, then finally managed to say the words. "I'm thinking about selling the bar."

That wasn't all he'd been supposed to say, but it was better than nothing. Still, Matthias's expression had turned stony. Parker wasn't surprised, but he also wasn't sure what to do about it.

"You're going to have to explain," Matthias said.

Parker rubbed the back of his neck. "There's not really an explanation. I think it's time for me to move on. I've always wanted to travel, and I think this is a good time to do that. I suppose I could keep the bar, but there's not really a reason to if I don't know how long I'll be gone. And if I sell it, I'll have money for plane tickets and whatnot."

Matthias was always scarier when he was expressionless. It meant he was pissed beyond normal and possibly was about to explode.

"Let me get this straight," Matthias slowly said as if making sure Parker would understand him. "You want to sell your bar, the bar you've been working on for years, to travel?"

"Yeah. I mean, if I don't do it now, when will I, right?"

Matthias wasn't amused.

Parker had no idea what else to say, so he kept his mouth shut. Maybe he should have ghosted Matthias like he'd planned, but he hadn't been able to do it. He didn't want his best friend to wonder if he was alive or why he'd left. This way, Matthias would know he was fine, and maybe, they could even keep calling each other. Parker wouldn't be able to come back because Matthias would see the problem eventually, but it didn't mean they'd never talk again. Parker hadn't been ready to give up his only friend, and he still wasn't.

To Parker's horror, Matthias's chin trembled. He reached for him, unsure what to do or say, but Matthias took a step back.

"You're leaving me," he said.

Parker swallowed. "I'm not." The lie tasted awful. "You're my best friend, and that's never going to change. I'm not going to vanish into thin air as soon as I leave. I've just been wondering what else is out there, and I feel it's time for me to find out."

"You don't have to sell the bar and vanish to travel. You're talking about eradicating the roots you have here. It means you wouldn't have a reason to come back."

Parker wanted to drag Matthias into a hug, but he knew better than to touch him when he was like this. "I just thought it would be easier if I sold the bar."

"I'll take care of it if you don't want to work here anymore, but there's no reason for you to. Besides, you'll be tired of traveling eventually, and you'll need a home to come back to. You'll need a job, too, so it's better if you keep the bar." Matthias's eyes widened. "Or I could go with you. My sister could take care of the bar permanently. You know she's great at it."

She was. Jasmine had been working for Parker since he'd

opened the bar, and he'd be lost without her. He'd been thinking about giving her more responsibilities before he'd realized he'd need to leave soon. That was the only reason he hadn't talked to her about it, and while what Matthias was saying made sense and Parker would have jumped on it any other time, he couldn't this time around.

"Matthias, please," he begged.

Matthias shook his head. "No. You're not going alone. Whatever your plan was, it was stupid. I'm not letting you go, and I don't understand why you'd want to. I thought we were friends."

Parker rubbed his face. "We are. You're my best friend and the one person I can't live without."

"Then why are you doing this? I don't understand."

For the first time, Parker was tempted to tell a human everything. He wanted to tell Matthias that he could turn into a giant dragon. Parker wanted to tell him that even though he was decades older than he looked, he had no idea how old exactly he was. He wanted to tell his best friend that he didn't know who he was and that he'd had to invent himself and even give himself a name.

He just hoped that Matthias would believe him.

He opened his mouth, knowing he needed to start somewhere even though he didn't know where, but the door swung open. Parker turned to glare at it, hating whoever had interrupted him. He'd just found the courage to tell his best friend what was happening. Why did they have to bother him now?

"The bar's closed," he snapped.

That didn't stop the man from stepping in. The darkness of the bar meant that Parker didn't have a good look at him until the door closed behind him after a second guy followed him inside. Parker scowled, even though the guy was incredibly cute.

He had to be in his late twenties, possibly early thirties, with shaggy blond hair that needed a cut. He was looking around with wide eyes, carefully avoiding Parker's direction as if he was afraid of what he'd see. His slim body was tense, and his expression spoke of anticipation, possibly even fear, but Parker had no idea why.

But even though he didn't know the man, something was pulling him forward. Even stranger, his dragon had perked up at the back of his mind and wanted to take a better look at the man.

What was happening?

"The bar is closed," Parker repeated, gentling his tone.

Instead of leaving like anyone else would have, the cute blond took a step forward. "I'm sorry to interrupt," he said in a soft voice that sent a shiver down Parker's back.

For some reason, Parker felt like he knew that voice. He should recognize it, even though none of this made sense. "It's fine," he said gruffly. "But you'll have to come back to-night."

The man stopped a little distance away from the counter and finally looked at Parker. He paled and reached for the counter, grabbing onto it as he stared.

Parker was about to ask him if he was all right, but he didn't get the chance to. Before he could, the man leaned for-ward." Byron?" he asked.

Parker didn't know who he'd been before waking up in the forest, but the name gave him a jolt.

Had this man known him before?

Ansley didn't know where to start. Byron was staring at him as if he didn't know him, which would make sense if he'd been trying to stay away from Ansley all these years. He was probably about to kick Ansley out as soon as he recognized him, but Ansley needed to say his piece before he left. He'd never be at peace otherwise. Even more importantly, he wanted answers for the others.

Surely, even if Byron had decided he'd rather stay away, the others wouldn't have. Marlow especially would never have abandoned Jarvis, which was what had made the mages believe that something bad had to have happened to their dragons.

But Byron was standing in front of Ansley, staring at him as if he didn't know him.

Ansley licked his lips. "I'm sorry if I interrupted you, and I won't bother you for too long. I just needed to see if you were okay. You never contacted me or the others, and I thought something had happened to you. I'll understand if you don't want to see me, but I just needed to make sure you were alive and well."

Byron was still staring. Ansley couldn't look at him any longer, so he turned his attention to the other man standing behind the counter. He was cute, with a riot of brown curls that fell in front of his forehead but were cut short at the back and on the sides. His brown eyes were wide, and his lips had parted as if he were about to ask a question. He and Ansley were similar in height, and the man was just as slight, which made Ansley wonder if this was Byron's boyfriend. Surely, if Byron had a boyfriend, he'd have chosen someone who didn't look so much like Ansley?

But that wasn't fair. Ansley and this guy didn't actually look alike. They had a similar build, but that was where it ended.

"I think you're mistaken," the guy said. "There's no Byron here."

Ansley's heart broke. He took a step back, but Jarvis stopped him, pressing a hand against his shoulder. He gently pushed him forward again, and Ansley went, even though there was nothing he wanted less.

"Wait," Byron said. "Do you know me?"

Ansley stared. "Of course I know you."

"Was that my name before? Byron?"

"What the fuck are you talking about?" the other guy asked.

"Matthias, please," Byron said.

Matthias pressed his lips together and stopped talking, but he kept looking from Byron to Ansley with a puzzled expression. Ansley didn't know where to start, and he didn't understand Byron's question.

"Your name has always been Byron," he said.

"I wouldn't know about that. I have no memory of who I was before I woke up in the forest."

Ansley sucked in a breath, his brain trying to make sense of the words. Byron had lost his memory. Was that why he hadn't come back to Ansley? "You don't remember me?"

Byron shook his head. "I don't. I'm sorry if that offends you, but I have no memory of you."

More than offended, Ansley was confused. Was the memory loss the result of the spell Carlyle had cast? Had it affected all the dragons? It would explain why they'd stayed away. If they didn't know who they were and couldn't remember their mages, it would make sense that they hadn't come back.

But where did that leave Ansley? He needed to tell Byron about everything, but did Byron even realize he was a shifter? He had to, right? He wouldn't be able to hide that side of him from himself, or at least, Ansley didn't think so.

He looked back, but Jarvis looked as lost as Ansley felt. He hadn't expected this, either, and neither of them knew what to do.

"Can someone explain what's happening?" Matthias asked. "Parker isn't this Byron guy you're looking for." He looked at Byron. "Right?"

Byron sighed. "I honestly don't know. I woke up a while ago in the forest, all alone, and I didn't remember who I was. I built myself a new life as Parker, but it's possible that I was this Byron guy before."

Byron—or rather, Parker—was clearly keeping some things out of his explanation, possibly because Matthias was human. It meant Ansley couldn't explain what was happening in front of him, no matter how much he wanted to help Parker wrap his mind around it. He felt protective of his dragon, as was normal, and he wanted to find Carlyle and kick his ass for what he'd done to Parker.

"Would it be possible to talk to you alone?" Ansley asked cautiously. He didn't want to anger Matthias, especially if he was Parker's boyfriend.

After all these years, the thought shouldn't hurt as much as it did.

"I'm not going anywhere," Matthias snapped.

Parker touched Matthias's arm. "Please. I promise I'll tell you everything when I can, but if this guy knows who I was before, I need to talk to him."

Ansley cleared his throat. "My name is Ansley. I apologize for not telling you sooner."

Parker waved Ansley's words away in a gesture that was so familiar that it threatened to make Ansley cry. He'd finally found his dragon, but things had changed. Parker still looked like Byron, even wearing different clothes, but what about everything else? With no memories, Parker wasn't the man he'd been before. He'd lost everything that had made him Byron, and as he'd explained, he'd rebuilt himself as Parker.

Where did that leave Ansley?

Matthias huffed. "Fine. I'll go, but you're going to explain," he told Parker. "You'll tell me about this memory loss thing and about wanting to sell the bar."

"I never meant to hurt you," Parker said.

Matthias's expression softened, but his eyes still blazed with anger. "I know you didn't, but I *am* hurt and pissed. I need you to be honest with me."

"I'll be as honest as I can."

Matthias narrowed his eyes. "Don't think I didn't notice what you did there. We'll talk later since you need to talk to this guy. I expect a phone call as soon as the conversation is over. You're not getting out of giving me an explanation."

"I'll call you," Parker promised.

Ansley risked peeking at them, wondering if they were about to kiss. If they were boyfriends, it would make sense.

But instead, they stared at each other for a moment before Matthias nodded and turned. He stomped around the counter, then toward the door, pausing briefly with his hand against it to look back at Parker. Then he pushed the door open and stepped out. It closed with a thump, the sound final as it echoed through the empty bar.

Now, Parker's attention was all on Ansley.

"My name is Parker," Parker explained.

Ansley had no idea where to start. "Ansley. And this is Jarvis," he added, gesturing behind himself.

Parker slowly nodded. "You really knew me before?"

"We both did," Ansley confirmed.

"Did you tell Matthias to leave because you wanted to tell me about the dragon?"

Ansley sucked in a breath. He'd known Parker had to be aware of his dragon, but he wasn't sure if this made his explanation harder or easier.

He was about to find out.

Parker hoped he hadn't given his secret away to someone who had no idea what he was talking about. At least he'd kept it vague enough that he could brush it off if Ansley didn't know. He suspected that wasn't so, though. If Ansley really had known him before, he had to be aware of the dragon.

Or at least, Parker hoped that was the case.

He didn't know what to think. He'd wondered for years who he'd been before and what his life had been like, as well as whether he'd left people behind when whatever had happened had knocked his memory out. He hadn't known if he had a family, friends, or a significant other. He still didn't, but he thought he and Ansley must have been close. That would explain why Ansley had been so shocked to see him and horrified when Parker explained he didn't have any memories.

Parker could only imagine how much it had to hurt. He didn't know if he and Ansley had only been friends or if there had been more between them, but either way, it had to hurt to have someone he'd clearly cared about tell him he had no idea who he was.

But what would Parker do if Ansley knew who Parker was and could explain it to him? He'd been planning on leaving anyway, and maybe now he'd have someone to go back to. It made him feel better, but only marginally. He'd still have to explain everything to Matthias, and he couldn't give his best friend a true explanation until he found out what he was dealing with. Once he had all the information, he could make a decision. For now, he was just confused and needed Ansley to start talking.

"Why don't we sit down?" Parker said, gesturing toward the tables.

Ansley looked relieved, possibly because they were taking more time. He didn't seem to want to tell Parker what had happened to him, and that made Parker wonder if it had been traumatic. He hadn't been wounded when he'd awakened, but he'd been dirty, sweaty, and exhausted. He'd always believed it was because he'd had an accident of some kind and ended up walking to where he'd woken up, but now he was starting to feel it had been something bigger.

"I'm going to go outside and call the others," Jarvis said.

He was talking to Ansley, but Parker could hear him anyway. He had better senses than humans, which was something he'd discovered along the way. In the beginning, he hadn't known what being able to become a dragon meant. He still wasn't sure why he was this way or if there was an explanation, but he'd gotten comfortable with both his forms, and he could shift between them seamlessly. The dragon was the only thing he'd carried with him from his past, and he'd always been grateful to have him. Now, he wondered if the dragon knew Ansley and if he'd missed the man.

"You should stay," Ansley said, sounding a little desperate.

Jarvis shook his head. "This is something *you* need to do. I'll be right outside if you need me, but you can do this."

"I don't think I can."

Jarvis squeezed Ansley's shoulder. "I have faith in you. You never gave up hope we'd find them, and you were right. You're the reason we're here and the reason we'll find the others. I'm proud of you, and I know the others are, too."

Ansley looked like he was about to cry. Parker decided to give the two men some space, so he went to the fridge to grab a few bottles of water. They were still talking softly by the time he reached them, and he offered Jarvis one of the bottles.

The man smiled at him and took it. "Thank you. As I was telling Ansley, I'll be right outside. I have an important phone call to make." He hesitated. "I can only imagine how confusing all of this is to you. I only ask you to listen to what Ansley has to say and give him the benefit of the doubt. You already know you're a dragon shifter, but that's only a part of what you have to learn."

"I'm not sure this is helping," Parker teased.

Jarvis laughed. "Maybe not. Just know that a bunch of people out there have been missing you for a long time and are overjoyed to have found you."

So maybe Parker did have a family somewhere. Maybe now that Ansley and Jarvis had found him, he'd get his family back.

He didn't want to hope until he had more details.

He waited until Jarvis left to turn to Ansley, who'd sat at the nearest table and was bouncing his knee. He was carefully avoiding looking at Parker, but knowing what he did now, Parker wasn't offended. He'd clearly been important to Ansley, and since he couldn't remember, Ansley was lost.

Parker sat in front of Ansley and placed the remaining two bottles of water on the table. He gestured at Ansley to take one of them, and Ansley did, his fingers shaking. He opened it and drank half of it in one go. Parker wanted to push but didn't think that was the best idea. Whatever Parker had forgotten, whatever the reason he lost his memories, he could tell it had been awful. He was almost afraid to find out, and while he didn't want Ansley to have to relive those memories, he needed him to. It was something big to ask of someone, especially someone he couldn't remember.

He leaned forward. "Take your time," he murmured. "But when you're ready, I have questions."

The corner of Ansley's lips curled. "About the dragon?"

"In part."

"Why don't you tell me what you remember?"

That wasn't why Ansley was here, but he was giving himself a little time, and Parker could give him that, even though he was curious. "Just that I woke up in the forest. I was in my dragon form and surrounded by trees. When I opened my eyes, the trees were all I saw, and it took me a moment to realize that I couldn't remember who I was. I didn't even know my name was Byron until you said it earlier."

"That must have been awful."

"It was, especially when I left the forest and realized I didn't know where to start. I didn't have anything, just the clothes I was wearing." Parker frowned. "About that. How is it possible for me to keep my clothes on when I shift? In all the books and movies, the clothes rip apart."

For some reason, that made Ansley smile. "It's magic."

Parker snorted. "Yeah, right."

"I'm not kidding. You're a dragon shifter thanks to magic. It's the same magic that gives you the ability to shift while keeping your clothes on, and believe me, you should be happy about that. I can think of several occasions that would have been incredibly awkward if you'd shifted naked."

Parker leaned back. "You need to tell me what's going on. The only thing I know for sure is that I can turn into a dragon. I had to rebuild myself a life, and I have to do it every so often because I don't age. Every time, I lose the people I care about, and I don't want that to continue. I don't want to lose Matthias, but I would like to know what I left behind. Can you tell me?"

Parker hoped Ansley would be able to. He still felt drawn to the man, even though he didn't understand why, but he didn't have to know why. Maybe it was because Ansley was part of his past, or maybe there was more to it. Whatever the reason, that wasn't what he was worried about right now.

He just wanted to know who he was.

CHAPTER THREE

Ansley didn't know where to start. He hadn't expected Parker not to remember anything about his past or what they were to each other, and it would be a lot to explain. He didn't want to overwhelm Parker, but he wasn't sure that was possible. With Parker not remembering anything, this wasn't going to be easy.

Ansley tightened his hands around the bottle of water Parker had given him. He stared at it, picking at the label with his nails. It gave him something to focus on that wasn't Parker, which he needed if he had to do this.

Maybe he could get Jarvis to come back. Hell, he'd even take Matthias, even though he still wondered if the man was Parker's boyfriend. Parker didn't want to lose Matthias, and they clearly were close from the way they'd behaved earlier. Ansley was glad Parker had someone after he lost his memories, even though it hurt.

But he and Parker had never been anything to each other beyond mage and dragon. It didn't matter that Ansley had been in love with Parker since they first met. Even after Parker had vanished from his life only a year later, Ansley had carried a torch for him. It was stupid, but it hadn't just been sustained by love. Parker wasn't just a guy. He was Ansley's dragon, his shield. The magic had chosen them for each other, and Ansley had always believed that eventually, Parker would come around and see that Ansley was perfect for him.

Clearly, Ansley had been wrong.

"Ansley?" Parker asked. He reached for Ansley's hand but

stopped before touching him.

Ansley was relieved. He was pretty sure he'd break down in tears if Parker touched him.

"Since you clearly don't know where to start, how about I ask questions?" Parker offered.

Ansley nodded. "I'll answer if I can," he promised.

"How about we start with my name? Was it really Byron?"

"Yes."

Parker wrinkled his nose. "I don't feel like a Byron."

"I suppose you're not anymore. You're Parker now. Everything that made you Byron is gone and has been for a long time."

"It has. I've been drifting around the country for a hundred years. Every ten years or so, I have to move because people start noticing I don't age. I was trying to explain to Matthias that I needed to go when you came in."

That got Ansley's attention, and he sat up straighter. "He doesn't know you're a dragon?"

"Not yet. To be honest, I was afraid to tell him. I've never told anyone, but no one has ever been as important to me as he is. I don't want to lose him, but I can't stay."

Parker's words reinforced the fact that he and Matthias were probably together, but Ansley didn't dare ask for confirmation. "I'm sorry you were alone for so long. I've been looking for you since you vanished, but I've only managed to find you now."

Parker stared for a moment. "What about you and me?"

Ansley sucked in a breath. "What about it?"

"Were we friends? Maybe something more?"

Considering how much time had passed, it shouldn't hurt as much as it did, but Ansley's heart felt like it was breaking. He hadn't known what to expect when he'd found Parker, and it was good to know that Parker hadn't stayed away because he'd wanted nothing to do with Ansley, but now,

Ansley would have to tell him everything.

He cleared his throat. "So you're a dragon shifter," he explained instead of answering Parker's question. "Magic exists, and it's the reason you can turn into a dragon. I don't know if magic created shifters, but it's what everyone believes, and I suppose it makes sense."

"Are you a dragon shifter, too?"

"No. I'm a mage. I can use the magic that surrounds us, and I do. Every mage has a shield. A protector who keeps an eye on them during fights or when the mages are casting spells. It takes a lot of focus, and usually, we lose track of what's happening around us. It's why magic pairs us with a shield."

Parker slowly nodded. "So the reason I'm not aging is that I'm magic."

"Pretty much. Dragon shifters live hundreds of years. They age extremely slowly."

"What about mages? Because I've been like this for about a hundred years, and if you knew me before, it means you haven't aged, either."

"Magic sustains us. It takes a bit of work in our case, but it's easier when we have our shields with us." This was hard. Byron had been born into a dragon clan, and he'd always known this, at least before Carlyle's spell. When he and Ansley had first met, Ansley hadn't needed to explain any of this. Byron had known.

But Byron was gone. Parker was in his place, and he wasn't the same man. Ansley didn't know how to behave or feel, but he had his shield back, and no matter what, that meant something to him.

Parker tapped his fingertips on the table. "You're the one explaining this to me," he said.

Ansley had no idea where he was going, but he nodded. "Mages usually live alone, but a small group of other mages and I banded together way back then to take down an enemy. We've been trying to find our shields since you all disappeared after the fight, and I've made seeking spells my specialty over the years. I was the one who found you."

Parker looked straight at Ansley. "Is that why you're the one talking to me, or are you doing it because I'm your shield?"

It made sense. Maybe Ansley was talking to Parker because he'd been the one to cast the spell, but that didn't sound right, and Parker didn't think that was the reason. Considering how Jarvis had left them alone, there was only one explanation why Ansley was here.

Parker was his shield.

Parker didn't know what to make of that. He'd never been anyone's protector that he remembered. He wouldn't know where to start, although he supposed he could protect someone fairly easily as long as he shifted into his dragon.

What was he supposed to protect Ansley from? The shields were clearly needed in battle, but how often did that happen? Had Parker missed something, or were mages so well hidden that no one knew about them and the fights they went through?

Parker still had many questions, and he wasn't sure Ansley would answer them. Ansley was staring again, apparently in shock, and Parker understood how he felt. The news that they were linked by a bond he didn't remember made him uncomfortable. How was he supposed to protect Ansley? Did he *have* to do it, or was there a way out of it? Parker didn't want Ansley to get hurt, but he wasn't sure he could do this. He didn't remember anything from his past, not even Ansley, even though he felt like he should.

Ansley cleared his throat. "Yes," he confirmed. "You were

my shield back then."

"Not anymore?" If mages needed shields, it would make sense that Ansley would have another one. It was a relief, but it also made Parker feel slightly angry. He was the only one who should protect Ansley, and his dragon agreed.

"I suppose it depends on you. I and the other mages have lived without our dragons since the battle. We've been looking for you all this time, and there was no way for us to know that you'd lost your memories. I assume it's been the same for all the dragons we lost, and it's a relief to know you didn't all stay away because you didn't want anything to do with us. We've been hiding in our home for decades, protecting ourselves as we could. We're vulnerable without our shields, but it doesn't mean you have to come back if you don't want to. We just wanted to know you were all right, and now that I've seen you, I can tell you are."

Parker still didn't know what to say. Ansley was trying hard to make him feel like he had a choice, but he wasn't sure that was true. If they were destined to work together, his place was with Ansley, especially since Ansley didn't have another shield. It didn't matter that Ansley's life wasn't as dangerous as it had been before. Parker's duty was still to protect him.

Or at least, it had been. Was it still? Parker wasn't the same person he'd been when all of this had happened. He wasn't Byron.

He rubbed his face, not knowing where to start. He was a bit scared because he'd never told anyone he was a dragon shifter, yet here Ansley was, aware of all his secrets. Ansley could use them against him, and while Parker didn't think he would, he needed to deal with it. He also had to decide what came next.

He'd been planning on leaving town anyway. He couldn't stay any longer without people starting to ask questions about why he looked so young. He hadn't chosen his next home yet, but he never did. It always hurt to leave his life behind, and he usually took several weeks to wander the country and try to find somewhere else to call home.

Where did Ansley call home? He'd explained he lived with other mages, and from the way he'd said it, it sounded like they'd been working together when whatever had happened, happened. "Why did I lose my memory?" he asked. He felt like his brain might explode if it got more information, but the silence was starting to feel heavy, and he needed answers.

"Jarvis had an apprentice," Ansley explained. "Carlyle was great with magic. But he felt like mages weren't respected enough. He wanted more than hiding in the shadows, and I understand why. Sometimes, I wonder what I'm doing. I can do incredible magic, but I spend my life hiding in a castle. Mages and magic have been in hiding forever, and not everyone is all right with that. Carlyle was one of those people who believed we deserve more, and he decided to take action. He grew his power using ways he shouldn't have to do things he shouldn't have done. He became a danger to the secrecy of our people, as well as to humans. We needed to act, and we did."

Parker wasn't surprised that a mage had gone mad with power. Thinking about what Ansley could do, even though Parker didn't have any idea of how it worked, was a bit scary. Ansley was well grounded, but clearly, this Carlyle guy hadn't been. Parker didn't know what Carlyle had done, but it couldn't have been good.

"He became more powerful than any of us," Ansley continued. "He killed hundreds of humans and tried to make himself the king of the world or something like that. I banded with other mages, and together we used magic to stop Carlyle."

Ansley's eyes fluttered shut as if he was thinking about what had happened back then. He probably was, and Parker had to resist the urge to reach for him over the table. He wasn't usually a touchy-feely person, but he wanted to touch Ansley. Since he wasn't sure it would be welcome, he kept his hands to himself and gave Ansley time to deal with the memories.

"I don't think I'll ever forget that final battle. We poured everything we had into it, and we won, but Carlyle had come prepared. He cast one last spell before we managed to trap him. He took our dragons away and, apparently, your memories. I suppose that he thought that this way, you wouldn't come back to us, and we'd be vulnerable when he came back."

"Wait," Parker said with a frown. "You didn't kill him?"

Ansley grimaced. "A few of us wanted to, but I would never have been able to do it, and Jarvis couldn't, either. Carlyle had grown up with him, and he was like a younger brother."

Parker wasn't sure what to say. He didn't know if he'd have been able to kill someone, but he didn't fully understand what had happened back then. He wanted his memories back, but something told him he'd never get them.

But he was angry at Carlyle. How dare the man take everything away from him? Parker had rebuilt his life, but he'd still lost so much. He couldn't remember anything, and maybe he never would. How was he supposed to deal with that?

Like he'd been dealing with it since he woke up. In the beginning, he'd hoped he'd get his memories back, but after a while, he'd accepted that it wouldn't happen. Maybe Ansley would be able to help, and maybe not. It wouldn't change anything. Parker wasn't Byron anymore. Even if he recovered his memories, he'd never be the man he'd been before again.

And maybe it wasn't such a bad thing.

"Why didn't he kill us?" Parker asked.

"You mean, why didn't Carlyle kill the dragons? It would

have taken a massive amount of magic. I suppose he could have done it with weapons, but dragon shifters are dangerous. You were highly trained to protect mages, and in a fight one-on-one with Carlyle, he would have lost if he hadn't used his magic. He probably would have won with magic, but there wasn't just one of you."

"How many?" Parker couldn't help but wonder how many dragon shifters were in the same situation he was in. How many men were out there, not remembering who they were?

"Six," Ansley whispered. "With you, we lost six dragons."

Parker leaned back. He was horrified at what Carlyle had done. Maybe it would have been better if he'd killed the dragons.

But no. Even though Parker had lost everything, he hadn't lost his life. He'd built himself a new one, and while he didn't know what he'd do now that he knew all of this, he had choices. He had a life, and he could decide how to live it.

"I know this is a lot," Ansley continued. "And I don't expect anything from you. Especially now that I know about your memories, I'll understand if you want to stay here. I'm nothing to you, and you don't owe me anything. You protected me when I needed it, and I needed to make sure you were okay, but now that I am, I can leave you to the life you've built here. You have people here, and I don't want to take that away from you."

"But you don't have a shield anymore."

"I don't."

"Can you get a new one?"

Ansley hesitated, then shook his head. "That's not how it works. You're alive, which means I won't get a new shield. I'm okay, though. Carlyle is trapped, and we haven't had to fight with anyone since the battle. You don't have to worry about me."

But Parker *was* worried.

It hurt to tell Parker he didn't need to come back. Now that he'd found him, Ansley didn't want to let him go, but he had to consider Parker's life. Parker wasn't Byron. He wouldn't be again, even if they somehow managed to unlock his memories. What he'd lived through since he'd become Parker had changed him, and Ansley wouldn't blame him if he decided to stay behind.

He wondered if they could get the memories back. Whatever Carlyle had done, Ansley had no doubt he'd done it maliciously. He suspected that even if they took years to study the memory loss and try to fix it, they wouldn't be able to. Carlyle was cruel, and he'd have made sure the mages regretted opposing him.

That was why he'd taken their shields. He'd wanted the mages to hurt over what they'd done to him, and he'd succeeded. It made them vulnerable at the same time, which was why they'd been hiding in their castle since it had happened.

But Ansley couldn't put this kind of responsibility on Parker's shoulders.

"I need time," Parker admitted. "What you just told me is a lot to wrap my mind around." He hesitated. "Do you think I could get my memories back?"

"I don't know. We've been studying the spell Carlyle used for decades, and we still aren't a hundred percent sure of what he did. He twisted the magic in ways he shouldn't have, and if that's the case, I doubt there's anything we can do to fix it."

Mages worked with magic. Magic wasn't a person, but it was a living entity. Ansley wasn't sure how to explain it to someone who couldn't feel it the way mages did, but to force the magic to do things it didn't want to do was something no mage should do. Carlyle hadn't hesitated, and he'd taken the magic, had twisted and hurt it. That was why the mages had stepped in to stop him.

They had, and they'd saved the magic and countless people, but they'd lost so much at the same time. None of them would ever want to twist the magic like Carlyle had. If that was what was needed to get the memories back to Parker and the other dragons, then, unfortunately, there was nothing they'd be able to do.

Parker nodded. "I expected that answer, but thank you for telling me."

"And thank you for listening to me." Ansley wanted to stay with Parker, but Parker didn't remember him. He couldn't remember how close they'd been, yet how far.

Ansley and Parker had still been trying to find their way around each other when Parker had been Byron. It often took mages and their shields years to be comfortable with each other, and they'd only had one. Ansley had always wondered how things would have gone between them if they had more time, but he wouldn't find out.

He missed his shield. He missed Byron, even though Byron had treated him like an annoying younger brother. He'd still been there for Ansley anytime Ansley needed him, and Ansley had thought they'd go back to that once they found each other again.

If Parker decided to come home, he and Ansley would need to build a new relationship. Part of Ansley couldn't help but wonder if they could have more than the bond between mages and shield this time. Jarvis and Marlow had been together and in love, and they hadn't been the only ones. Parker and Ansley had never been like that, but with Parker being different, maybe they could be.

Ansley bit his lower lip. He desperately wanted Parker to come to the castle, and he was terrified Parker would say no. He'd respect that decision, though, and he didn't expect

Parker to decide one way or the other right now.

So he pushed away from the table and got to his feet. Parker jerked back as if he'd been lost in his thoughts and hadn't noticed what Ansley was doing. He jumped up, looking around as if he expected a threat. Even though he didn't remember being a shield, it was ingrained in him.

"What's happening?"

"I should go," Ansley told him. "You need time to process what I told you."

"Are you going home?"

"I don't know." Ansley didn't want to, at least not until Parker had made his decision. "I need to talk to Jarvis."

Parker nodded. "But you're coming back, right?"

"If you want me to."

"I don't know what I want right now. Why don't you give me your number? That way, I can call you if I have questions."

Ansley was happy to do that. He left his number with Parker and had to pull himself away from the dragon. The magic wanted them to stay together, and it felt confused when Ansley reached out for it. He couldn't explain what had happened to Parker in words because the magic wouldn't understand, but he tried soothing it, hoping it would be enough. He didn't want it to try to force him and Parker together when Parker wasn't ready for that.

They stood there awkwardly, staring at each other. Ansley shuffled his feet, then finally moved toward the door.

"Call me if you need anything," he said.

"I will," Parker promised.

Ansley wasn't sure he could trust that promise, but he didn't have a choice.

The sun blinded him when he stepped outside, and he told himself that was the only reason his eyes prickled with tears. He rubbed them and looked around, trying to find Jarvis. It took him a moment, but when he noticed Jarvis on the other side of the street, he rushed to reach him.

He wanted to fall into his friend's arms, and he suspected Jarvis knew it just by looking at him.

"I grabbed us two rooms in a motel," Jarvis said.

"Why?" They could come back anytime they wanted using a portal.

Jarvis shrugged. "I thought you'd need time to be alone after what happened. I called the others, and they're freaking out. I told them we'd stay here until we could talk to Parker again. How did he take it?"

"He's confused."

Jarvis nodded. "Anyone would be confused in his place. Hell, *I'm* confused, and I have all my memories." He wrapped an arm around Ansley's shoulders. "Come on. You need some rest."

What Ansley needed was a safe place where he could break down and cry, and while he wouldn't have chosen a motel room to do it, that was what happened when he stepped into the one Jarvis had decided would be his. Thankfully, Jarvis came with him, and when Ansley's knees crumbled and tears came streaming down his cheeks, Jarvis was there. He grabbed Ansley, hauled him into his arms, and sat both of them on the bed. He held Ansley close, allowing Ansley to bury his face against his chest.

"He doesn't remember me," Ansley said with a sob.

"I know," Jarvis soothed. "It doesn't mean he won't want to come back."

But Ansley knew that Jarvis had the same fears he did. What if Parker didn't want to come back? What if he decided to stay here, with his new life and Matthias?

And what if the same thing had happened to all the dragons? What if none of them remembered their mages, and they decided to stick with their new lives rather than come home?

The door had barely closed behind Ansley when Matthias burst in, making Parker wince when the door slammed against the wall. Matthias looked around, nodded as if satisfied to see that Parker was alone, and strode in, slamming the door back shut. Parker glared at him.

Parker had sat at the table again, trying to make sense of what Ansley had told him, but he couldn't wrap his mind around it. He hoped that in time he'd be able to accept what had happened to him. For now, it was impossible.

"Who was that guy?" Matthias demanded to know. "What was he talking about when he called you Byron? Did you really lose your memory? I thought that only happened in romance novels."

Parker stared. He owed Matthias the truth, but could he give it to him? He'd been planning on leaving anyway, but he never wanted Matthias to look at him with fear in his eyes.

And that was if Matthias believed him. What if he thought Parker was going nuts? What if he decided he was better off dumping Parker so he wouldn't have to deal with any of this? There could be so many reasons for Matthias to decide he wanted nothing to do with Parker ever again, and Parker wasn't sure he could take that.

Ansley had known Parker before, but Matthias was Parker's only friend. He'd been Parker's family since Parker had moved to town, and he didn't want to lose his friend.

Matthias flopped into the chair Ansley had been sitting in and leaned forward. "Well? Should I start calling you Byron?" He wrinkled his nose. "That doesn't suit you."

Parker found himself smiling. "That's what I said. I don't feel like Byron."

"Are you sure that you *are* Byron? I mean, the guy could have been lying, right?"

Parker shook his head. "He wasn't. He knew things that

only someone who knew me before could tell me." Parker had never told anyone he was a dragon shifter, which meant Ansley had known it from before. It was as simple as that.

Matthias still didn't look convinced. "What things? What the fuck happened?"

Parker couldn't stand it if Matthias rejected him today of all days. Maybe he could give him part of the truth and keep the rest for later. Matthias wouldn't leave without an explanation, and Parker needed to decide how much he was willing to give him.

"I never told you this, but I lost my memory a while ago. I woke up alone in the forest. I had no idea who I was or what my name was." He didn't mention how long ago that had been or that he'd moved from town to town since then. "Eventually, I found my way here, chose a name, and settled down. I had no idea what I'd left behind, and I still don't know too many things. Ansley knew me before, though. We were friends, and he's been looking for me since I vanished."

Matthias frowned. "What happened to you? Were you in an accident?"

"Something like that. Ansley told me I was attacked. They caught the guy who hurt me, but I'd already wandered off, and they weren't able to find me."

Matthias stared for a moment, his eyes narrowed.

Parker wasn't sure what else he could give him today. He didn't have it in him to start a full explanation.

"I know you're hiding stuff," Matthias eventually said.

"He told me other things, but I can't talk about those right now. I need time. I believed I'd lost everything and that I'd never recover it. I still don't have memories, and I don't remember Ansley, but he gave me more details, and it's going to take me a while to wrap my mind around that."

Matthias's expression softened. "I can understand why. Why didn't you tell me what happened to you?"

Parker shrugged. "What would it have changed? You're my friend, even though I have no idea who I am."

"I don't care who you were before."

"Thank you, but I do."

"Did Ansley tell you that you were a bad guy or something?"

"No. He said I protected him, which is why I got hurt. Look, I promise I'll give you more details as soon as I can, but you need to give me some time." Parker got to his feet. He was ready for this day to be over, and it was only eleven in the morning. What was he supposed to do with the rest of his day? How was he supposed to be at work when he couldn't stop thinking about his past and what Ansley had told him?

Matthias stood up, too, and walked around the table. He wrapped his arms around Parker and squeezed, and Parker sank into the familiar gesture.

He might not remember who he'd been, but he'd never forget this. Matthias had been his friend for close to a decade, and maybe Parker would lose him soon, but for now, they were still friends. Matthias was the only steady person in Parker's life.

And it fucking terrified Parker that he might not be for much longer.

Matthias patted Parker's back. "Why don't you go home? I'll take care of the bar."

"You mean your sister will," Parker said, gently pushing Matthias away.

Matthias glared, only to smile immediately after. "I'll just do what she orders me to do. She's always been better than me at this. Don't vanish on me, though. You were talking about leaving town, but I don't want you to go until we've had a chance to talk about all of this."

"I'm not going anywhere for now." But Parker would have to, eventually. Even if he was honest with Matthias and

Matthias, by some miracle, accepted that he was a dragon shifter and immortal, Parker couldn't stay. Other people would start noticing he wasn't aging, and it wasn't something he knew how to deal with.

He didn't know where he'd go when he left. Maybe he'd follow Ansley, spend some time with him and the other mages, and hopefully find the other dragons. He'd never met another dragon shifter, but even though he had no memories of the other shields, he felt a kind of kinship with them. They'd probably lost their memories, too, and he knew how that felt. He'd lived it and wanted to help in any way he could.

Matthias elbowed Parker in the side. "You're not going to follow Ansley?" He wiggled his eyebrows. "Because he's cute."

Parker was glad for the way Matthias was able to pull him out of his thoughts. "He is," he agreed.

Matthias grinned. "Is he sticking around for a bit?"

"I don't know. He gave me his number, so I can call him, but I think we both need some time. I have no memories of him, and it's hard for me to wrap my mind around the fact that I used to know him and that we were close. I can only imagine what it's like for him to have me not recognize him. I lost everything, but I don't remember what that everything was. He lost me, and he knows who I was."

Even though Parker had decided he'd go home for now, Matthias had to push him out the door. Once he stepped into the parking lot, he tilted his face toward the sun, wondering what was next.

Luckily, he lived above the bar and had a good bottle of scotch hidden somewhere. Maybe he'd grab some food and get drunk. He didn't usually do that, but his mind was spinning, and he didn't know how to make it stop. Drinking wouldn't solve his problems, but for a time, it would help him take a step away from reality, and that was what he needed.

47

Besides, it wasn't like any of this would vanish because he was drunk. All his problems and Ansley would still be here, waiting for him tomorrow morning when he woke up with the mother of all hangovers.

CHAPTER FOUR

The sound of someone knocking echoed in Parker's head. He groaned and clutched at it, hoping the pressure would help, but he doubted anything could.

His hangover was there to stay.

He tried rolling out of bed only to lose his balance and fall next to it. His back hit something, and he realized he'd never made it to bed but had fallen asleep on the couch. He glanced around, glaring at the sun streaming in through the window. An empty bottle of scotch was still on his coffee table, along with the wrappers of the burgers he'd grabbed last night for dinner.

The knock came again. It could only be one person. Parker still had no idea what to do with Matthias, but clearly, the time had come for him to decide. He wasn't sure how he'd manage, considering his head was pounding and he couldn't think clearly, but he owed it to his best friend to be honest.

"What?" he croaked.

The knocking finally stopped. There was a pause, then the handle moved, and the door opened. Matthias peeked in, looking almost afraid. He relaxed when he noticed Parker by the couch, then frowned. "Why are you on the floor?" he asked as he came in and closed the door.

"Why are you here?" Parker asked instead of answering. He pushed himself up onto the couch, his stomach sloshing.

"I brought you breakfast."

Parker blinked up at Matthias, and sure enough, he was holding a paper bag that smelled heavenly. Parker's stomach

49

growled, and his dragon pushed him forward. They needed food, and they needed it now.

Matthias laughed and dropped the bag onto the coffee table. "Eat. I'll start the coffee pot."

As much as Parker knew they needed to talk, he'd feel better doing so once he had his hangover under control, so he obeyed. He tore through the breakfast sandwich, the warmth and grease settling his headache. By the time he was done, Matthias was back with a steaming cup of coffee, which Parker took with a grateful smile.

Matthias sat next to him, his entire body so tense that Parker was surprised he wasn't vibrating.

"Whenever you're ready," Matthias said.

Parker sighed. "You're not going to let this go, are you?"

"Hell, no. How can I? I deserve answers, both about your past and what you plan to do in the future. You were going to leave me yesterday. Has that changed?"

Parker hesitated, then shook his head, instantly regretting it. It felt like his brain was rattling around, and he pressed a palm against his forehead, silently begging it to stay still.

Thankfully, Matthias could tell how bad Parker felt, and he gave him a moment to gather his thoughts.

"Okay," Parker eventually said. "I'm going to tell you everything."

Matthias leaned closer. "Everything?"

"Everything I remember, anyway." Parker had been thinking about it since meeting Ansley, and he'd made his decision. Whatever happened next, he couldn't stick around. When it came to Matthias, he only had two options. Either he told him the entire truth, or he kept his mouth shut and vanished. Matthias might believe he was going nuts if he told him he was a dragon shifter, but Parker could show him the truth. If Matthias ran away screaming, Parker would deal with it. He knew his best friend, and Matthias would never tell anyone about this if Parker asked him not to. The only thing that could happen was that he'd decide he didn't want them to be friends anymore, and Parker could deal with that.

Or at least, he hoped he could.

He licked his lips. "You know we've been friends for almost ten years, right?" he started.

Matthias frowned, then nodded. "I haven't forgotten."

"You've changed a lot over those ten years. You've aged."

Matthias scowled. "Are you trying to tell me I look old?"

"No." Parker couldn't stop himself from smiling. "I'm just trying to tell you to look at me. Have I changed during those ten years?"

Matthias cocked his head and stared. "Well, you let your beard grow. I'm still not sure I like it, by the way."

Parker wanted Matthias to take this seriously, but he understood why his friend wasn't. He just had no idea how to explain what he was, so maybe the best thing would be to go straight to the point.

"I haven't grown older," he blurted out. "For the past ten years, I've looked this way, and it's not going to change. It hasn't changed in a hundred years since I woke up in the forest."

"That can't have happened so long ago," Matthias interrupted. "You're only in your mid-thirties."

"Are you sure? Because the first memory I have is from a hundred years ago."

Matthias's mouth dropped open. "That's just not possible. You'd be older if that was the case."

Parker opened his arms. "I don't know how old I am. I promise I wasn't lying when I told you that I woke up and didn't remember anything, not even my name. I'm glad I have it back, even though he doesn't feel like me anymore, but I'm even happier that I finally have answers."

"I don't understand anything you're saying. Are you sure

you're okay? How much did you drink last night?"

Parker grabbed one of Matthias's hands and squeezed. "Listen to me, all right? And please, keep your mind open. I swear I'm not lying, and I know you trust me."

"Of course I trust you." Matthias squeezed. "You're the best friend I've ever had. You wouldn't lie to me."

Parker swallowed. "But I *have* been lying to you. I didn't tell you the entire truth. I wasn't human when I woke up all those years ago. I was a dragon, and since then, I've been able to shift back and forth. I'm a dragon shifter, Matthias."

Matthias stared. Parker wasn't sure what else to tell him or how to explain, but maybe it would be better to give Matthias a few seconds to digest the news.

"You mean like in fantasy books or something?" Matthias eventually asked.

"I guess." Parker wasn't much of a reader.

Matthias's frown deepened. "So you can turn into a dragon."

"I can."

"And you're sure you're not still under the influence of the stuff you drank last night?"

"I promise I'm not. I shouldn't have drunk as much as I did, but the only thing left is a headache."

"And you swear you're not lying to me?"

"I do. I can show you if you want."

Matthias looked around the room. "Unless you're a pocket-sized dragon, I don't think it would be the best idea to do that now."

He wasn't wrong, but Parker was desperate for his best friend to believe him. Once he did, he'd either accept Parker or run away screaming, and while Parker wasn't looking forward to finding out which way Matthias went, at least then he'd know.

He opened his mouth, but Matthias raised a hand in front

of his face, effectively shutting him up. Parker obeyed the silent order, knowing he needed to give Matthias time. Hell, he probably needed to give him a bottle of scotch, although Matthias being human meant he'd be in even worse shape than Parker if he drank all of it.

Matthias was silent for a moment. Parker knew he'd made a decision when he nodded at himself and turned his attention back to him.

"Okay. What about everything else?"

"What do you mean?"

"Well, I'm guessing you wanted to move because you're not aging, and people will start to notice eventually. I haven't, but maybe it's because I spend so much time with you. Anyway, I want to know about Ansley. Who is he? Another dragon shifter?"

Parker breathed easier. "You believe me?"

"Of course I do. You promised you're not lying."

"You're not afraid of me?"

Matthias snorted. "Why should I be? Correct me if I'm wrong, but you've been a dragon shifter the entire time we've known each other, right?"

"I have."

"But you never hurt me. I don't see why you should start now that I know your secret. Now tell me about Ansley."

Parker did. He blurted out everything, needing his best friend's support. He still had no idea how he felt about what Ansley had told him or what his next step would be. At least now, he could be honest with Matthias, put all his cards down, and ask for help.

Matthias listened, silent, keeping his questions for the end. He didn't have many of them, at least not that Parker could answer. Unfortunately, knowing who he'd been before hadn't given Parker his memories back.

Once Parker was done talking, Matthias straightened his

back. "Well, wherever you're going, I'll be coming with you."

"I can't ask you to do that. Your entire life is here," Parker protested.

"Then it's a good thing you're not asking me to go with you. I'm coming, and that's final. I'm not ready to lose you, especially if you decide to go with Ansley. I mean, I'm sure he's a nice guy and everything, but you don't know him. He could be a serial killer and lock you up in his dungeon as far as you know."

Parker laughed. He doubted Ansley was a serial killer, but if he decided to follow Ansley home, it would be good to have Matthias with him.

Parker suspected he'd need at least one familiar face to get through whatever Ansley threw at him next.

Ansley was usually a morning person, but today, he wanted nothing more than to stay in bed. He was afraid of what the day ahead held for him, and he didn't feel ready to face it. Unfortunately, he didn't have a choice.

Now that he'd found his dragon, things should have been smooth, but that couldn't be further from the truth. The situation was more complicated than any of them had expected, and to be honest, Ansley wasn't sure how to deal with it. It would be easier to stay in bed and hide from the world, but Jarvis knew him too well, which was why Ansley wasn't surprised when his friend pulled the curtains away from the window to allow light in the room.

"Come on," Jarvis coaxed. "It's getting late."

Ansley grabbed his pillow and pressed it against his face. "Who cares?"

"I do, and I'm pretty sure Parker does, too. He'll want to talk to you."

"What if I don't want to talk to him?"

Ansley couldn't see Jarvis's expression, but he could imagine it all too well. His friend would be worried but also slightly disappointed in how Ansley was behaving. Ansley couldn't deny he felt like a child right now. Considering how old he was and how long he'd been working on finding Parker, he should be happy and ready to roll with the punches. Even though Parker didn't remember him and had no idea what his life before had been, he was alive, and he hadn't left Ansley behind because he wanted to. That was supposed to be a win, right?

Maybe it was, but it still felt like Ansley's heart had been torn out of his chest, and he had no idea how to put it back.

It didn't even make sense. He and Parker had been nothing more than friends before, if even that. If it had only been Parker missing, Ansley would have thought the dragon had decided to stay away. He wouldn't have been surprised.

But he'd known that wasn't what had happened because of the others. Marlow would never have left Jarvis behind. They loved each other, and he wouldn't have abandoned Jarvis and left him vulnerable, even with Carlyle gone—and the dragons had vanished before Carlyle had been trapped, so none of them would have known he'd been dealt with. Now, they knew why the dragons hadn't come back, which was kind of horrifying.

Ansley couldn't begin to imagine what it was like not to remember anything. Parker had lost his entire life from before, and he'd had to build himself a new one with no knowledge of what he'd left behind. Ansley wasn't sure who had it worse, the mages or the dragons. Thankfully, it wasn't a competition.

The mattress dipped next to his hip, and a gentle hand grabbed his shoulder. "I can only imagine how you feel," Jarvis murmured. "But you did it. You found one of the dragons, which means you can find the others, too. If all of them have lost their memories, it's going to take a lot of work to get them back. It wouldn't have been possible without you, Ansley, and I don't know how to thank you."

Ansley pushed away the pillow and glared at Jarvis. "Stop that."

Jarvis appeared amused. "Stop what?"

"Being so nice and shit. I'm trying to mope, and you're making it hard."

"I apologize. You realize you've given me the one thing I wanted most in the world, right?"

Ansley sighed. He did realize that, and he wanted to find Marlow. Out of all of them, Jarvis was the one who deserved to find his shield the most.

Maybe that was what Ansley was supposed to focus on. Clearly, this mess with Parker wouldn't be easy to get out of, but Ansley could ignore it.

Right?

Ansley patted Jarvis's hands. "I'm fine," he promised.

"You're far from fine, but I'll act as if I believe you. I think you need to talk to him. Hiding away isn't going to help either of you, and he has questions. Didn't you promise to give him answers?"

"I already told him everything there was to know. He's aware of the past we share, what happened, and why he lost his memories. I told him what we are to each other, and he asked for time to think about things. That's what I'm giving him. He doesn't need to see me again so soon."

"I'm pretty sure that's not correct, but he's not the only one you need to talk to." Jarvis took out his phone, and dread filled Ansley.

He'd known he needed to talk to the others. They were aware of what had happened yesterday since Jarvis had called them to let them know, and just like Jarvis, they were happy to know that the spell actually worked. They wanted their dragons back, and Ansley wanted to give that to them.

He just hoped their reunions would be better than his with Parker.

Ansley didn't try to stop Jarvis from making the call. He wasn't sure who he dreaded talking to the most, but in either case, he didn't have a choice. He might as well get at least this out of the way.

"Jarvis?" Penley's voice echoed in the room. Jarvis had put them on speaker, dammit.

"Is everyone there?" Jarvis asked.

"Yes. We've been waiting for you to call. What took you so long?"

"That would be me," Ansley said with a groan. He sat up against the headboard, hugging his pillow. He needed to get through this conversation. That was all. Everything else, he could focus on later.

"Why? What's going on?"

"He's being slightly dramatic," Jarvis said with a smile. "You know Ansley."

"When can you start looking for our shields?" Tyne interjected.

Ansley glared even though his friend couldn't see him. "I'm still trying to deal with finding mine. You could give me a little more time."

"You've had years."

"I think that what Tyne is trying to say is that we're all inpatient but happy to know that your spell worked," Dallin said.

Ansley had to resist the urge to run and hide, maybe in the bathroom. Would Jarvis follow him there?

He didn't blame his brothers. The mages had been looking for the dragons for decades, and this was the first time they came anywhere close to one of them. He was still stunned by the fact that the spell had worked, and if he allowed himself to think about it, the situation wasn't as dire as it could have been.

Parker hadn't stayed away because he'd wanted to. He'd stayed away because he didn't remember Ansley, which meant he hadn't abandoned him. He hadn't had a choice, and wondering what he would have done if he did was pointless. Ansley would never find out, and it didn't matter.

"I'll be home as soon as possible and cast the spell again," Ansley promised.

"How long is it going to take him to pack?" Tyne asked.

"I don't know. To be honest, I'm not even sure he'll want to come."

There were a few gasps on the other side of the phone, and Jarvis squeezed Ansley's knee.

"What do you mean?" Keyon asked.

He'd always been the quietest of them all, and for him to speak meant he was truly worried. Whether it was because he wondered if his dragon would want to stay away or because he didn't want Ansley to get hurt, Ansley didn't know. It was probably a mix of the two.

Ansley sighed. "He has a whole life here and doesn't remember me. I wouldn't blame him if he wasn't ready to leave everything behind," he explained.

"That's bullshit," Tyne snapped. "He's your shield. Of course he'll want to come."

"I hope so, but I wouldn't blame him if his answer was no. He knew he wasn't human before today, but he didn't know anything about magic, and being a shield is a lot of responsibility. He feels lost, and I don't blame him."

Ansley's phone vibrated on the nightstand. It wasn't one of his brothers, but it could be Etta, so he snatched it up to peer at the screen. His jaw dropped open when he read the text he'd just gotten and realized who it came from.

I'm coming, but Matthias will be coming with me.

It wasn't a question. Parker was telling Ansley that Matthias would be coming with them, and it was implied that if

Ansley said no, Parker wouldn't be going anywhere. Ansley wasn't sure he wanted Matthias there, but he realized it was only because he was jealous. He wanted Parker to himself, but that clearly made Parker uncomfortable, and he needed someone he knew to be there. Ansley didn't blame him. It didn't matter if Matthias was Parker's friend or his boyfriend. It wouldn't be fair to ask Parker to face all of this alone, and Ansley wouldn't.

He cleared his throat. "It looks like Parker made his decision," he said.

"Is he coming?"

Even though Ansley had no idea what would happen or if he'd be able to deal with any of this, he found himself smiling. "He is."

CHAPTER FIVE

Every time Parker moved, he realized he'd accumulated more things than he was supposed to and than he'd expected. He didn't know what to do with half of the stuff in his apartment, but he would have to decide.

He hadn't known what to expect when he'd texted Ansley that he was coming but wouldn't be coming alone. Matthias had thought the mages would tell him he had to stay, and Parker wouldn't have been surprised if they had. Instead, Ansley had agreed that Matthias could come, had told Parker there would be more than enough space for both of them, and had suggested he start packing. He'd made sure to tell Parker that they could come back for anything he left behind, but Parker wasn't sure he needed to move all of his stuff to wherever they were going. He certainly didn't need to do it right away, so he'd packed a backpack with the essentials he'd need once he arrived at Ansley's home. He was putting everything else in boxes, but he was having a hard time choosing what he had to leave behind.

He'd been supposed to start packing a while ago. He'd already known he'd be moving on, even though he hadn't expected any of this to happen. He still wasn't sure what to expect from Ansley and the other mages, but for the first time, he was actually excited at the thought of moving. Maybe it was because Matthias would be with him, or maybe because of Ansley and what his presence meant. Parker didn't know and didn't want to examine his feelings too closely.

He grabbed his backpack and went outside to put it in his

truck. Ansley had told him to pack everything he needed and put it in his vehicle, and Parker wondered if they were about to go on a road trip. They had to get to this place somehow, right? Ansley hadn't been mysterious on purpose, but rather, he'd been avoiding Parker. Parker wasn't sure how that was supposed to work, since his job was to protect Ansley, but he was relieved he wouldn't have to start doing that right away. He wouldn't know where to start.

He considered going back upstairs to grab a few more things when he noticed Jarvis and Ansley coming toward him down the sidewalk. He leaned against the side of his truck and waved, and Ansley waved back hesitantly. He looked like he expected Parker to tell him to fuck off, which made Parker wonder what kind of guy he'd been before.

Ansley was adorable. When Parker was around, he always seemed to be flustered, and it made Parker want to wrap him in his arms and never let go. Ansley was clearly trying to keep some distance between them, and every time, it was as if he expected Parker to react poorly to their closeness. Parker didn't like feeling like an asshole, and that was what it made him feel like. He'd have to talk to Ansley about it, but he suspected Ansley wouldn't be honest, so maybe it would be better to talk to Jarvis.

Ansley just wanted Parker to come home, as he called it. Parker could tell he'd do pretty much anything to make that happen, even hide the truth from him. It wouldn't be fair. Parker didn't need to be coddled. He needed to be told everything, even if his old self had been a dick.

But they had time. He'd met Ansley only two days ago, and things had been overwhelming enough as it was. He could find out more about his old self once they got to Ansley's home.

"Good morning," he said with a smile when the two men reached him.

Jarvis's smile was open and happy, while Ansley's was more hesitant. "Good morning," he said. He peered at the truck. "Is that all you're taking with you?"

"You said we could come back later, and I didn't want to be a burden."

Ansley shook his head. "You won't be, and you can get more things." He eyed the truck, then turned to Jarvis. "You're sure you can make the portal big enough for the entire truck?"

"It won't be a problem," Jarvis promised.

Parker's brain was stuck on the portal thing. "Portal?" he asked, hoping for an explanation.

"It's how we got here," Ansley told him. "My specialty is seeking spells, while Jarvis's is portals. He can open them pretty much anywhere and make them as big as he needs them to be."

Parker blinked. "Is that something you can do, too?"

Ansley shrugged one shoulder. "In a pinch, I can get us out of a bad situation, but I'm not nearly as good as Jarvis. Once, I ended up in the wrong country." He grimaced, and Parker grimaced with him because that didn't sound good.

"You can drive your truck through the portal," Jarvis assured. "We'll be coming back for the rest of your things, but we're not sure when. We have to be careful not to draw too much attention, and the portal I need to open today is a big one. So fill your truck as much as you can. That way, we'll have fewer things to move when we come back."

It made sense, and Parker was glad he'd started packing up his things in boxes. That way, he wouldn't have to waste time.

He made several trips, carrying boxes down the stairs to fill his truck. By the time he was sure he had most of the things he'd need, Matthias had joined them. He and Jarvis were talking, and Parker took a moment to listen to them. He couldn't believe Matthias was coming with him, or maybe he could. He should have known his best friend wouldn't let him leave on his own.

"She's been working at the bar for years, almost since it opened," Matthias was saying.

He was telling Jarvis about his sister and how she'd be the one taking care of the bar. Parker didn't think he'd ever come back, which meant he should probably sell it, but Matthias had insisted on giving Jasmine some time to show him she could do this. Maybe once she was used to being in charge, she'd want to buy the bar. That would be perfectly fine with Parker, and it wasn't like waiting would change anything for him.

All of this was overwhelming. Parker was leaving everything he knew behind, and considering he didn't know what he'd find where he was going, it was a massive risk. It was good that he wasn't doing it alone, but he couldn't help but worry. What if he ruined Matthias's life? What if this was the wrong decision to make?

"I'm ready when you are," he said.

Matthias grinned at him and grabbed his hand, squeezing hard. "Can you believe it? Jarvis said he was going to open a portal. I feel like I'm in a movie."

Matthias sounded more excited than Parker at the thought of what they were about to do, and Parker found himself smiling. This was an adventure, and to be honest, Parker couldn't wait to see what awaited them on the other side of the portal. He was glad he wouldn't have to do it alone and that Matthias was excited. It helped him remember that whatever had happened in his past, the important thing was what would happen in his future. He couldn't change the man he'd been before, but he didn't think he was a bad person now, and he wanted to show Ansley that. He might not know what he was doing, but for some reason, he was Ansley's protector, and that meant something to him. It was one of the reasons he'd agreed to go with Ansley and Jarvis, and he hoped things would work out.

"Ansley?" Jarvis asked. "Can you cast a spell to hide us?"

Ansley nodded. Parker stared at him, curious to see magic, and he didn't miss the way Ansley avoided looking at him. He'd make sure that changed, and soon. He didn't like Ansley being intimidated by him, especially when the opposite should be true. Parker could turn into a dragon, but Ansley's gift was even more impressive. He could use magic Parker hadn't even known was there. He represented both Parker's past and his future, and it hurt that he was staying away.

Parker would have to make sure that changed.

Ansley was very careful not to look at Parker, although he'd failed spectacularly in the beginning. Parker had been alone when he and Jarvis had first arrived, and it had felt safer to peek at him. Now that Matthias was here, it was better if Ansley stayed away, which was what he intended to do.

He had a job, so he focused on that. They couldn't go back to the forest, since they were taking Parker's truck with them, which meant that Jarvis had to open a portal here in the alley. Thankfully, they were behind the bar, fairly hidden from the main street, so they should be okay. Still, it would be safer to cast a spell so no one would notice them, which was what Ansley was supposed to do instead of thinking about Parker.

Ansley sucked in a breath and closed his eyes. He reached out to the magic, and it rushed toward him as if it had been expecting him. Sometimes, he wondered if the magic missed him, but he wasn't sure he'd ever get an answer to that. He also wasn't sure he needed one. The magic was what it was, and there was no changing it. Whether it was excited to feel him or not, the result would be the same.

He pulled on the magic and molded it until he had what resembled a shield. It would let things pass through, but no one would see them. They were hidden, and the people walking past would only see an empty alley.

Ansley opened his eyes to nod a Jarvis. "It's in place."

"Good." Jarvis stared ahead.

When he raised a hand, Matthias sucked in a breath loud enough for Ansley to hear him. Ansley bit his lower lip, not wanting to snap. Of course Matthias was amazed. He hadn't known magic existed until yesterday. He'd accepted it as if it had always been part of his life, which was a surprise, but Ansley supposed that Matthias was ready to accept a lot of things if it meant keeping Parker.

The portal was a pinprick in the beginning, but it quickly grew. Ansley had seen this happen hundreds of times, yet the ease with which Jarvis did it always amazed him.

The portal looked like water. Unless someone touched it, it was placid and allowed them to see the other side. It meant Parker and Matthias could see they'd end up in a courtyard when they went through. They couldn't see most of the castle around it, and Ansley knew they'd be surprised. He was kind of excited to see them react to the castle, and he mentally scolded himself. This wasn't a game, and it wasn't a vacation. He was taking Parker home, where he belonged and where he shouldn't have left.

Sometimes Ansley dreamed of finding Carlyle and shaking him until his teeth rattled and fell out of his mouth. Ansley wasn't a violent person, but he could defend himself if he needed to. He hadn't hesitated to cast the spell against Carlyle, and he'd been glad they weren't killing him, but now that he knew what had happened to their dragons, he wondered if that would have been the best outcome.

It wouldn't have changed anything. Carlyle had cast his spell before they'd imprisoned him into the stone, where he still was. The dragons would still have been cast away, their memory lost.

But Ansley would have felt more satisfied at the thought that Carlyle had paid for what he'd done.

"We can go," Jarvis said, looking at Parker and Matthias.

Parker climbed into his truck, but Matthias hesitated. He seemed to want to step through the portal on foot, which was a perfectly fine thing to do. Jarvis gestured at him to go ahead, and Matthias stared at him with wide eyes.

"Our brothers have been warned you were coming with us," he explained. "They're expecting you, so you don't have to worry they'll attack you."

Matthias squeaked. "They could have attacked me?"

Jarvis chuckled. "Well, you're a stranger who will suddenly appear in our courtyard. They'd have been in their right to defend their home."

"I think I'll get in the truck with Parker."

Jarvis laughed as Matthias rushed to the truck and climbed into the passenger seat. Ansley almost rolled his eyes, but he could understand where Matthias was coming from. No matter how hard he was trying not to like the man, he couldn't stop it.

With a huff, he turned toward the portal. He continued staring at it as Parker slowly drove through it, Jarvis crossing right behind him. Jarvis looked back at Ansley, who quickly moved through the portal, dropping the spell he'd been keeping up so no one would notice them.

Ansley relaxed once the portal was closed behind them, but this was only the beginning. He watched as Parker and Matthias got out of the truck, their eyes wide as they looked around. He'd lived here for a long time, so he was used to the castle, but he tried seeing it with new eyes.

It was impressive. The courtyard was right in the middle of the castle and was one of four. All around them were stone walls, and it could feel claustrophobic. The castle had been built like this for a reason, though, and that reason was dragons.

The courtyards were wide enough for the dragons to shift and take flight while being protected by the walls. That way, if the castle was attacked, the dragons would be safe shifting in and out of their dragon form. Tyne had added plants, trees, and flowers to the courtyards, so it was softer, but the castle was still built to withstand an attack, and there was no hiding that, no matter the number of flowers.

"You didn't tell us you lived in a castle," Matthias exclaimed.

"I apologize," Jarvis told him. "To us, this is home, and we don't think much about it."

Matthias looked at him like he was nuts. "It's a castle."

"It is, and it's your new home."

Matthias looked stunned. Ansley was, too. Jarvis had basically told Matthias that he could move in with them, and while Matthias wouldn't be the only full human who lived there, he was still an unknown person. Ansley wanted to ask Jarvis what he was thinking, offering that, but he didn't dare.

He knew himself. He was jealous of Matthias because of how close he was to Parker, which meant he'd have to keep himself in check. He didn't want to make Matthias uncomfortable, or worse, send Parker running. He had no doubt that was precisely what would happen if he didn't treat Matthias right, and even though it was hard for him to see Matthias and Parker together, he'd have to get used to it.

Dragons and mages didn't have to be together, although it often happened. Parker didn't owe Ansley anything, especially not a relationship. They'd never been together that way, and Ansley hadn't expected that to change even if he found Parker. What did it change, then, to have Matthias there? It meant Parker was more comfortable, which was all that mattered in the end.

It still wasn't easy to accept, but Ansley would have to deal with it. As of right now, the castle was home to Parker and Matthias, too, and Ansley had no right to want them out.

But that didn't mean he had to be there and watch them. It didn't mean he had to torture himself that way, and now that they were home, he could take a moment to himself. He took a step back, then another, just as Parker turned toward him, a smile on his face. The smile went straight to Ansley's heart, and he forced himself to look away.

Even though Parker was nothing like Byron, he still looked like him. It was hard to reconcile the two, and Ansley wondered if he would ever be able to. Would he expect rejection every time Parker looked at him?

Only the future would tell, and for once, Ansley wasn't eager to find out.

Parker wanted to tell Ansley to stop, but he didn't feel he could. It wasn't his place to ask Ansley to stay with him, at least not yet. He'd have to tread carefully if he wanted Ansley to get used to having him around and to relax in his presence, and that wouldn't be done over just half an hour.

So Parker watched as Ansley walked away, even though he wished he could go with him. He watched him until he disappeared behind a door, and only then did he look around.

He understood why Matthias was still staring at the place where they'd landed after crossing the portal. It was almost like a fairytale for someone who'd always lived in small towns. For Parker, too, because he didn't remember any of this.

The courtyard was big but made to look smaller by the wooden columns supporting awnings and passages high on the walls. Everywhere Parker looked, he saw stone—the walls, the ground, the imposing archway, and the three ramps of stairs leading inside the castle. Wooden benches lined the walls under the awnings, surrounded by a riot of flowers and plants that made the place look less like a place that belonged in the middle of a war. They scented the air, making it smell sweet and welcoming even though the place was imposing.

The door Ansley had disappeared through was slightly to Parker's left, its massive stone archway imposing. The two windows next to it were high and pointed at the top, the glass crisscrossed by black lines. They, too, looked like they belonged in a medieval castle, as did the other windows Parker could see. One was encased in a stone frame that reminded him of an ancient cathedral. The grated metal door next to it helped with that impression. The sky was open above them, a shocking blue that made Parker blink.

The sound of footsteps made both Parker and Matthias look up. One of the staircases ended by the door Ansley had taken and led up to another door protected by an awning. The door was open now, and a group of men was coming down the stairs so quickly that Parker expected at least one of them to tumble down. He stepped forward as if he could do something to stop it, then caught himself and stayed where he was.

"Byron!" a cute blond said as he threw himself at Parker.

Parker caught him—what else could he do? He wrapped his arms around the guy, holding him close, and to his surprise, emotion flooded him. He didn't remember this man, but something about him was familiar, enough that he buried his face against the man's hair and breathed him in.

"Don't keep him all to yourself," a voice grumbled.

The blond stepped back, but he didn't let go of Parker and grabbed one of his sleeves as if he was afraid that Parker would disappear otherwise.

Parker turned to the man who'd spoken. He had long brown hair that he impatiently pushed behind his ears and teary brown eyes. He was more hesitant, but when he opened his arms to hug Parker, Parker found that he wanted to be hugged. He pulled the man into his arms, holding him tight.

As soon as they were done, a third man was there. Parker didn't hesitate to drag him closer like he had the others. Clearly, they'd missed him, and even though he didn't remember them, it felt like his soul had missed them.

This guy had short, dark hair with red tips and warm brown eyes. He was as tall as Parker, which meant Parker was able to bury his nose against the man's neck and take a deep breath. His dragon cooed in the back of his mind, and Parker suspected it would be doing a happy dance if he were to shift now.

The last guy didn't try to hug Parker. He was taller than Parker, with broad shoulders and dark hair so short that Parker wouldn't have been able to run his fingers through it. The man stared at him with hard, dark eyes, and Parker wondered if maybe, not everyone was happy for him to be back.

That wouldn't stop him. He offered the guy his hand and waited to see what would happen. The guy stared at it, then, to Parker's relief, took it. Parker was stunned when instead of shaking his hand, the guy pulled him closer for a quick hug and a pat on the back.

"I don't get hugs?" Matthias suddenly asked, getting everyone's attention.

Jarvis laughed. "I'm sure that at least a few of them will hug you if you ask. Why don't I introduce you first?"

"That would be great," Parker agreed. He felt like he knew these men, but he couldn't even remember their names.

"Everyone, as you know, this is Parker. He doesn't go by Byron anymore, so maybe try to remember that."

The first guy's cheeks flushed. He'd called Parker *Byron*, but Parker didn't mind, even though he didn't feel like Byron. Byron was the man these guys had known, and it made sense for them to call him that. He expected them to slip up at least a few times, and he didn't care if they did.

"The blond who assaulted you is Penley," Jarvis continued. "This is Dallin," Jarvis said, pointing at the second guy. "Then we have Keylon, and finally, Tyne."

It felt good to place the names and associate them with a face. Parker smiled at all of them, feeling like he was finally home, even though he didn't understand it.

He didn't have to understand. His dragon knew they were home, and that was all that mattered.

"This is Matthias," Parker said, introducing his best friend.

"Where's Ansley?" Keylon asked, looking around.

Jarvis frowned. He seemed older than the rest of them but not as grumpy as Tyne. If Parker had to guess, Jarvis was in his late thirties, with Tyne being in his early thirties and the other three in their twenties.

Of course, he was probably wrong, considering how old *he* was. It was what they looked like, though, and it was easier to think of them as being in their twenties rather than wonder how old they truly were.

"He left before you got here," Jarvis said.

Penley frowned. "Why? He should be with Byron." His cheeks flushed. "Sorry. That's going to take some time to get used to."

Parker shook his head. "It's fine. I understand where you're coming from."

"We really didn't expect anything like this. I mean, we knew something had to have happened, since our dragons never returned, but memory loss? I've been looking into it and trying to find a way to fix it, but so far, I've come up empty."

Parker smiled, hoping it was a reassuring gesture. "That's fine. I've gotten used to being Parker, and while it would be easier to know what I'm supposed to do here, I'm fine as

Parker."

"So is Matthias your boyfriend?" Dallin asked.

Parker blinked, but before he could answer, Penley stepped in.

"He can't be Parker's boyfriend. Parker is supposed to be with Ansley."

"They weren't before."

"Maybe not, but it doesn't mean they won't be now. They're mage and dragon. It's how it works."

"Try not to overwhelm Parker," Jarvis said. "I'm sure he and Matthias want to see the castle. I'll show them to the guest rooms."

Penley looked disappointed, but he let them go. Parker's mind was stuck on what Penley had said, though.

Were he and Ansley supposed to be together? That would explain why Ansley had run as soon as they'd arrived and why he always looked away when Parker tried to get his attention. Parker hadn't realized that dragons and mages were supposed to be a couple, but he supposed it made sense. He didn't have memories of him and Ansley being together before, but Dallin had said they hadn't been. Had Ansley expected that to change now that he'd found Parker again? Did he think Matthias was Parker's boyfriend?

Parker sighed. The only way to get answers to those questions would be to ask Ansley, but something told him it wouldn't be that easy.

Ansley knew he should stay with Parker. The dragon was surrounded by people he didn't know, and he'd be a bit lost. Ansley couldn't bring himself to spend any more time with him, though. It had nothing to do with Matthias and everything to do with the fact that Parker didn't recognize him.

Ansley rushed through the hallways toward his office. He

knew what he had to do, and it wasn't crying over the fact that Parker didn't know who he was. He'd finally found a spell that worked, which meant he could start finding the other dragons. His brothers expected him to do everything he could to find their dragons, and considering the kind of relationship they had with their shield, their reunion would probably go better than the one between Ansley and Parker.

Even though Ansley and Byron had never been close, Ansley had imagined the day they'd find each other again so many times that he'd lost count. The two of them were destined to be together, chosen by magic, and he'd always trusted that. Even when he'd believed Byron had stayed away because he wanted to, he'd thought he'd be able to change the man's mind.

Everything was a mess. Byron wasn't Byron anymore, and Ansley had no idea what to do with Parker. They should spend time together and get to know each other again, but how could he do that? When Parker looked at him, he didn't recognize him. He didn't know Ansley or how to behave with him, and Ansley didn't blame him.

So he'd stay away. He didn't need a shield anymore. Carlyle was trapped, and he wasn't going anywhere. Sure, not knowing where the stone was worried Ansley, but they'd find it eventually. It would be easier once they had the dragons back, and that was what Ansley would focus on. He'd found a spell that worked. That meant he could find his way to the other dragons and give them back to his brothers. He wasn't happy, but they could be, and in the end, that was all he wanted.

He was a bit jealous at the thought that they'd finally be reunited with their dragons while he planned to stay away from Parker, but he'd get over it. It wasn't like he needed to spend time with Parker. It was good to have him around just in case, but Ansley doubted that Parker would have to protect him from anything worse than a stubbed toe or a paper cut. The world had changed, and most mages didn't seek power anymore. They wanted to be left in peace to live their lives, just like Ansley and his brothers.

They were giving Parker an opportunity he normally wouldn't have had — to find out more about his past and what he could do, to tell Matthias what he truly was — but that was where things ended. Parker didn't need Ansley, and Ansley didn't need Parker.

Or at least, that was what he was trying to convince himself of.

He turned the corner and almost collided with Thorne, who was coming toward him. The housekeeper reached out to grab Ansley, but Ansley took a step back, hitting the wall with his shoulder. He felt like if anyone touched him right now, he'd break down into pieces.

"Everything okay?" Thorne asked.

Ansley forced himself to smile. The housekeeper worried about all of them, but he didn't need anyone interrogating him. "I'm fine."

"I heard you were coming back with your dragon." Thorne looked around as if Ansley were hiding Parker somewhere. "Where is he?"

"Still in the courtyard."

Thorne frowned. "Yet, you're here."

Ansley resisted the urge to snap at him. Thorne meant well, and he was a friend. "I needed some space. It's a lot."

Thorne's expression turned to understanding. "Oh, of course. You've been looking for him for so long that now that you found him, you're overwhelmed. I'm sure he'll understand."

"He does." Ansley had no idea if that was so, but he didn't want to open his heart to anyone, not even Thorne.

The housekeeper was in his mid-forties, and he'd been

taking care of the mages for nearly two decades. He was human, but he knew what they were and what they could do. Penley kept asking him to allow them to use magic to stop him from aging, but Thorne had refused so far. Ansley didn't know why, and he'd never asked. He felt it was none of his business, and Thorne had been told that if he ever changed his mind, he could go to any of them, and they'd help. They all loved him like a brother, even though it had been strange to watch him age while they stayed the same. Ansley didn't want to lose Thorne, but it was his choice, a choice all of them respected.

"You're going to your office?" Thorne asked.

"Yes. I thought I'd work on the spell for a while, since it's fresh in my mind."

"I'll bring you something to eat."

"You don't have to."

"Maybe not, but I want to. You and your brothers would be starving if it weren't for me taking care of you."

That much was true. "I won't say no to a sandwich."

Thorne clicked his tongue. "Maybe some soup, too. You need nutrition, maybe a vegetable or two."

Ansley found himself smiling, even though, on the inside, his heart was bruised.

He'd get over it eventually. He just needed his heart to realize that Parker wasn't within his reach and that that was okay. Parker belonged with Matthias, and Ansley needed to dash the hope he'd had that things could change between them. He hadn't been able to do so when he'd found that Parker had lost his memory, but it was clear Matthias was important to Parker. He wouldn't have brought him here otherwise.

Ansley would find the other dragons and continue working on the spell to find the stone where Carlyle was trapped. Once all of that was done, he could dedicate himself to his studies or something else.

And so what if his dragon wasn't really his?

CHAPTER SIX

Parker had enjoyed meeting the other mages, but he was glad when Jarvis guided him and Matthias into the castle. He needed some peace and quiet, and he wouldn't get that with the mages around. Well, Tyne wouldn't be a problem, but Penley? He hadn't stopped talking since they'd met, and he hadn't given any sign he would. He was enthusiastic and happy that Parker was back with them, which touched Parker in a way he didn't quite understand.

Maybe it was because in the life he could remember, he'd never had anyone like that. He had Matthias, but beyond him, he'd never had brothers, people who wanted him around and who were happy to see him. He might not be related by blood to Penley, but Penley clearly saw him as a brother, and while it was odd, it also warmed Parker's heart. He hadn't known what to say when he'd agreed to follow Ansley home, but he could already tell it was the right choice. Coming to the castle would give him a lot more than he'd have had if he'd left on his own as he'd done in the past.

"You have to excuse the others," Jarvis said.

"I'm not angry at them."

"Good. When they were told Ansley found you, they were incredulous but happy. We were always the closest to our own dragon, but we're a family, you know? We want all the dragons found, and not just because they belong by our sides. We've missed you, even though you can't remember it."

Parker felt slightly guilty that he couldn't remember. He realized it was stupid and that there was nothing he could do to change it, but he couldn't imagine how Ansley and the others felt. They had an image of him in their mind, a knowledge of the man he'd been before, and it had to be hard to wrap their mind around the fact that he wasn't that person anymore. It was hard for him to accept the fact that they'd known him when he didn't even know himself.

But there was no changing that, and he didn't *want* to change it. He didn't have to be the person he'd been before to be part of this family and to get to know the mages. He'd find his footing with them, and they'd already shown they were ready to welcome him as if he'd never left. It was overwhelming, but it felt good.

"What about Ansley?" Parker asked.

He didn't miss the glance Matthias shot him, but he ignored his friend. He was curious about the mage who was supposed to be his, especially after the way Ansley had run as soon as they got to the castle.

Jarvis sighed. "I know he left, but it has nothing to do with you."

"It seemed it had everything to do with me."

"Well, with the old you and the expectations Ansley had."

"He said we were never together. He mentioned that usually, dragons and mages end up being couples, but that we never were."

"That's correct."

"Were you and the other mages dating your dragons?" Parker wasn't sure how to feel about that. It didn't sound like they were forced to be together, but rather like the bond between mage and dragon pulled them together in a way that ended up in love. It wasn't a bad thing, just strange to think about.

"Most of us," Jarvis confirmed. "Marlow and I were together the longest. Tyne and his dragon were still dancing around each other, but we all knew they'd eventually end up together. They had a kind of push-pull relationship, but that had a lot to do with Peyton's family. Penley and Devon were cautious in their relationship, but I have no doubt they'd have ended up together eventually."

"But not Ansley and me?"

Jarvis grimaced. It felt like whatever he wanted to say, he didn't want to hurt Parker, which was enough to tell Parker it wasn't good. He didn't know anything about his old self. He couldn't remember the man he'd been, but he couldn't understand how he could have hurt Ansley. He didn't like feeling like he might have been the kind of person who would do something like that.

"You hadn't known each other that long, just a year. I'm sure things would have smoothed out eventually," Jarvis explained. "And I wouldn't worry too much about Ansley if I were you. He's overwhelmed and wants to work on finding the other dragons, but as long as you give him enough space, he'll come around."

Parker wanted to ask more, but he wasn't sure Jarvis would tell him, and he was overwhelmed enough as it was. He couldn't find out everything about his past today or even this week. It would take time for him to wrap his mind around the person he'd been and accept that he would never be that person again.

From what he was starting to find out, it wouldn't be a bad thing.

So instead of asking more questions, Parker focused on their path. He felt they'd been walking for hours, and he was pretty sure he'd get lost if he tried finding his way back to the courtyard, but then, the place was massive. Everywhere he looked, there were light gray stone, archways, and columns. There was artwork on the walls and carpets on the floors, which made the castle almost homey, but with so much space, it was hard to make sense of everything.

Jarvis eventually stopped in front of a door. They'd climbed two flights of stairs and were now in an empty hallway. Several doors opened on it, and if Parker had to guess, they led to guest bedrooms.

"This room and the one in front of it are at your disposition," Jarvis explained. "It doesn't matter which one of you takes which room. I hope they'll become your home, eventually."

Parker didn't know what to say to that, so he nodded. When Jarvis pushed open the door, Parker stepped inside, his eyes widening at the sight in front of him. "I don't need so much space."

Jarvis smiled. "All of the rooms are like this. Make yourself at home."

This wasn't just a guestroom. The door opened on a sitting room, and since there was no sign of the bed, Parker guessed it meant it was in another room. This room had one wall covered with bookshelves and wide windows that opened onto a lake. Parker had seen the lake from the windows as they walked through the castle, but he had a better view from here, and it looked incredible.

There was a fireplace on the opposite wall, with a thick carpet in front of it, a table, and several couches and armchairs. The room was decorated in dark wood, greens, reds, and browns, and it made him feel right at home, even though he'd never been here.

"That door leads to the bedroom, and from there, to a bathroom," Jarvis explained. "This other door leads to a small office. Feel free to use all the space. We have a housekeeper, and I'll make sure to introduce you to him as soon as possible. He'll want to know what you enjoy eating and your schedule so he and the others won't bother you cleaning."

"I can clean by myself."

"I have no doubt that you can, but Thorne is very

particular. He enjoys taking care of us, and he takes pride in that. I wouldn't anger him if I were you."

Parker had no intention of doing that. He nodded, his gaze attracted to the windows. Jarvis chuckled when Parker took a step toward them, said something to Matthias, and the next thing Parker knew, the door was closing behind him.

He looked back at Matthias, whose eyes were as wide as his felt.

"I have to say that for a while, I thought all of this was bullshit," Matthias said. "Then he opened the portal, and I kind of freaked out."

"You can go home." Parker didn't want him to, but he wouldn't try to stop him.

"Hell, no. I'm not going anywhere while you're living in a freaking castle. Do you think my room is as big as this one?"

If Parker had to bet, he'd say yes.

He flopped onto one of the couches and looked around again. He didn't understand how his life had changed so much over just a few days, but he was used to rolling with the punches. He'd find a way to get used to this, too.

He had to.

Ansley wasn't surprised when someone knocked on his office door about an hour after he and the others had arrived at the castle. He'd just finished eating the soup and grilled cheese Thorne had brought him, and he'd been about to start working.

Well, he'd been about to start working the spell itself. He'd been going over a few notes, so his mind was already focused on work.

But he couldn't avoid Jarvis forever. His friend would push until he could make sure Ansley was okay, which meant Ansley had to open the door. He didn't want to, but there was no way out of it, so he got out of his chair and went to open it.

"Tyne?" Ansley asked, looking around for Jarvis.

Tyne huffed and pushed past Ansley. "What? You think I don't care about you?"

Tyne had always been a little gruff, which Ansley didn't mind. He knew Tyne cared, no matter how hard it was for Tyne to say the words. "I know you do."

Tyne crossed his arms over his chest and stared at Ansley. Since this was clearly going to be a conversation, Ansley closed the door, wondering what Tyne wanted.

He could imagine, even though it wasn't like Tyne to want to talk about this.

"You left," Tyne said.

And there it was. "I did. You wanted to talk to me?"

"No. I wanted to see you and your dragon together."

Ansley winced. "Parker and I aren't together."

"You weren't before, but it doesn't mean that things can't change."

"I don't expect them to."

Tyne snorted. "Bullshit. I know you hoped when you found him again that you'd be able to convince him the two of you belong together."

"Well, clearly that hope was dashed, and I don't want to talk about it."

"Did you tell him how you felt?"

"No. Why would I?"

"Because you've been carrying a torch for him for a hundred years. The least you can do is acknowledge that."

"But don't you see? I haven't been in love with Parker all this time. I was in love with Byron, and he doesn't exist anymore."

"He's still the same person."

"I don't think he is." For one, Parker had never treated

Ansley like he was a bother the way Byron often had. It was one of the things that had given Ansley hope, but with Matthias here, he couldn't allow himself to hope any longer.

"Well, I hope he's less of an asshole. You really should talk to him, though."

Tyne was doing this because he cared, but it was annoying. Ansley didn't want to talk to Parker. What was he supposed to say? He couldn't just tell him he'd been in love with Byron and that he wanted to climb into Parker's bed. Parker didn't know him, and he didn't know Parker. He'd hoped things would be different, and maybe they would, but for now, he felt it was better to stay away.

"He's already dealing with enough," he said, hoping his tone would tell Tyne to steer away from this topic of conversation. "I have no intention of pushing my feelings onto him, especially since he can't remember me. He doesn't need this, too. He'll need time to get used to living here and what all of this means, and I don't want him to have to worry about my feelings."

"The two of you should be together."

"Maybe, maybe not. Dragons and mages don't always end up together, and that's fine. I don't need to be with him to be happy to have him back. He's safe, and that's all that matters to me. I won't demand anything he can't give me."

"You don't have to demand it. You just have to be honest."

"I will." Eventually, maybe. Ansley didn't see the point of telling Parker he'd been in love with Byron. There was nothing Parker could do about it, and Ansley didn't want to make him uncomfortable.

Parker needed to get to know the other mages, explore the castle, and make sense of the life he'd lost and the one he was gaining. It was all Ansley wanted for him.

What he wanted for himself didn't matter.

CHAPTER SEVEN

Over the past few days, things had been incredible. Parker had done his best to settle down, and it hadn't been easy. He'd gone from living alone to living with a bunch of people he barely knew, and the only reason they weren't driving him nuts was that there was plenty of space for everyone to be alone if they needed it.

And he had, often.

The only person Parker kept close was Matthias. He was familiar, and it helped Parker feel anchored. Parker's old life felt almost like a dream, but he had no memories of being Byron, and he had a hard time putting all of it together. He'd talked to the mages, who had told him about Byron and the relationship they'd had with him, but he didn't recognize himself in what they said. Tyne, especially, had seemed pissed when he'd told Parker how Byron had treated Ansley, and Parker understood. He didn't sound like he'd been a nice person, and he hated that this was the memory Ansley had of him.

Maybe that was why Ansley stayed away. If he expected Parker to behave the way he had when he'd been Byron, it would make sense that he'd decided to keep his distance. Parker didn't blame him. Honestly, he probably would have done the same in his place.

But he didn't want Ansley to think he was like Byron. After everything that had happened to him, he wasn't the same person anymore, and he liked the man he'd become. He wanted to show Ansley that he'd changed, but how could he, when

Ansley had been avoiding him?

Parker hadn't seen him once since he'd arrived at the castle a few days ago. He'd expected to during meals, but apparently, he'd had the housekeeper, Thorne, bring food to him. Of course, that was when he remembered he needed to eat, but it looked like Thorne was good at taking care of the mages, which was a relief. It wasn't Parker's job to make sure Ansley was okay, but he couldn't stop himself from wanting to do just that. When he mentioned that to Jarvis, Jarvis had pointed out that his job was literally to protect Ansley, even from himself.

Parker had decided that something needed to change. Ansley couldn't continue to hide from him, and he was ready to face whatever fucked-up relationship they'd had before. He was also ready to find out what his job was supposed to be. He was Ansley's dragon, his shield, which meant he was here to protect him.

But from what?

It would be easier to get answers if Ansley wasn't avoiding him, but Parker didn't just have Ansley to talk to. There were other mages, and just like Ansley, they knew what his job was supposed to be. They'd be able to give him pointers and explain what they expected from him.

Tyne was intimidating, and Parker was pretty sure the mage would rather throw him out the window than spend any length of time explaining anything to him. Penley was sweet, but he tended to get lost when explaining something, so he was out, too. Dallin and Keylon would be fine, but Parker already knew Jarvis, so he'd decided to go find him.

He still got lost when he tried finding his way through the castle, but thankfully, Thorne had given him a map. He felt a bit ridiculous, almost like a tourist, but if this was what he needed to find his way around his new home, he'd use it.

Thorne had written down what the rooms were and where

to find the mages—except for Ansley—so Parker knew how to get to Jarvis's office. That was where he headed, and even with the map, he almost got lost a few times. By the time he got there, he was antsy and couldn't wait for the conversation to be over. He wondered if maybe he should go back to his rooms and take a few minutes, but the need for this conversation wouldn't vanish. He had to talk to someone, and if it couldn't be with Ansley, Jarvis was the second-best option.

Luckily, Jarvis seemed to enjoy talking to Parker. When he saw Parker at the door, he waved him in with a broad smile. Parker was slightly uncomfortable, but he was glad that at least someone was happy to see him.

"What can I do for you?" Jarvis asked as he sat behind his desk.

Parker looked around. The room was decorated similarly to the rest of the house, with a lot of dark wood and fall colors. Jarvis's office was neat as a pin, though. Everything was in its place, and the objects on the desk were perfectly symmetrical. It was a bit much and not how he'd imagined Jarvis's office.

But he wasn't here to talk about the way Jarvis furnished his office. "It's been a few days since I arrived, and I'd like to talk to someone about what I'm supposed to do," he explained.

"I'm not sure I understand."

"Well, I'm a shield, right? What do I have to protect Ansley from? What do I have to be careful about? And more importantly, can someone teach me how to fight? I'm sure Byron could fight, but I don't know where to start."

"I have to admit I didn't think of that."

Parker shrugged. "I didn't in the beginning, either, but I've had some time. I'm here for a reason, and I don't want to disappoint Ansley."

"I don't believe anything you could do would disappoint him."

From what the others had told Parker, he'd gotten the impression that while Ansley had always believed he'd hung the moon, Parker, as Byron, hadn't always been nice to Ansley. He wanted that to change, but he didn't know how. Maybe showing Ansley that he was ready to protect him—as he should—would help.

Jarvis sighed. "This is a conversation you should have with Ansley. I realize you want to know about the past and what happened between the two of you, but I can't give you those answers."

"I understand, but he's been avoiding me. I don't even know where he spends most of his days."

"That would be in his office. Do you have the map?"

Parker's cheeks heated, but he nodded and took it out of his pocket. Jarvis was smiling when he took it, stared at it for a moment, then grabbed a pen and drew a cross. For some reason, Thorne hadn't written down where Ansley's office and his rooms were, and Parker was sure that had been intentional.

"You'll find him here," Jarvis explained, pushing the map toward Parker. "He's going to tell you everything is perfectly fine and that you have nothing to worry about, but don't believe him. We're all worried about him. We thought that finding you would help, but it has brought up difficulties we hadn't expected."

Parker didn't know what to say. "Was I an asshole to him before? When I was Byron, I mean?"

"You weren't the nicest man. I'm sure that would have changed, though. Remember that you hadn't had a lot of time together and that a year is nothing, considering dragons are basically immortal. I've been with my dragon for a long time, but the first few years were shaky." Jarvis's smile was fond as he thought of Marlow.

Parker knew the two of them had been in love and hoped

Jarvis would find him soon. It didn't feel fair that Parker been the first to be found.

But at the rate Ansley was working, he'd probably have all of them at the castle by next week.

"Give yourself a chance," Jarvis said. "You're not Byron anymore, and as far as I can see, that's a good thing. Whatever you went through after losing your memory changed you, and you and Ansley have to learn to deal with that. He remembers Byron, but he doesn't know Parker. Maybe you should show him you're not the same person anymore."

"I want to. I'm just not sure he'll allow me to."

"You'll have to push through the shields he put up. He's always been like that, but especially so since we lost the dragons. He's been so focused on finding you that he forgot how to live. Maybe having you here will change that."

Parker wasn't sure, but he had to do something. Talking to Ansley would be the easiest thing to do and a good start.

As long as Ansley gave him a chance, anyway.

Ansley wanted to work. He wanted to find the other dragons, but for some reason, the spell hadn't worked when he'd tried it again. He'd focused on Marlow this time because he felt he owed it to Jarvis, who'd been there for him every step of the way, but nothing had happened. The map hadn't changed. That made Ansley wonder if the spell didn't work anymore, if it had only worked because he'd been focusing on his own dragon, or if Marlow was out of the country. All of those things were possible, and he'd have to experiment to find out which one it was.

Maybe he could start searching for the other dragons. Out of all of them, at least one had to be in the same country, right? But he really wanted to do this for Jarvis, and he knew the others would agree that he needed to be the next one to get his dragon back.

Unfortunately, that was proving to be harder than expected.

The fact that Ansley kept getting distracted by thoughts of Parker didn't help. He still couldn't believe he'd found his dragon and that Parker was in the castle, going about his day while Ansley was trying to work. What was he doing right now? Was he even thinking about Ansley? Or was he spending most of his time with Matthias?

Ansley wouldn't blame him. If Ansley had a boyfriend, he'd be spending a lot of time with him, too. Unfortunately — or maybe luckily considering his job — he didn't have anyone, which meant he spent all his time working.

He sighed. He'd thought his reunion with Parker would be different, although he should have realized it wouldn't. He and Parker had never been close, not even when Parker was Byron. Really, what had Ansley expected? Had he thought Parker would throw himself into his arms? That they'd finally have the possibility to be together?

He should have known better. His life hadn't changed, even though his dragon was in it again. He was still the same old Ansley, and that was never going to change, Parker or no Parker. Really, Ansley should have attempted to find his dragon last, not first.

He glared at the map in front of him on his desk. Why wasn't it working? Why wasn't it showing him where Marlow was? Ansley hoped he wouldn't have to change the spell, and there were a few things he could try before doing so. He got up, turning to his shelves. He needed a bigger map, one that included other countries. That way, if Marlow was in another country and that was the problem with the spell, Ansley would be able to find him.

A quick knock on the door made him glare. He didn't need anyone bothering him, but unfortunately, they all knew where to find him. They never hesitated to knock on his door, and while he hadn't minded until now, he really needed to be left alone.

A second knock told him that wouldn't happen. He groaned and glared at the door. "What?"

The door opened, and Etta peeked in. "Don't use that tone with me," she scolded.

He winced. "Sorry. You know how I get when I'm working."

"We all do, which is why we try not to bother you. The new guy clearly didn't know."

She could only be talking about two people, and there was no way Matthias was here to visit Ansley. He didn't have a reason to. "Is Parker here?"

Etta grinned. "He is, and let me tell you, you're a lucky, lucky man."

Ansley's cheeks flushed, and he looked away. "I'm really not. We're nothing to each other except mage and shield."

"But the others all dated their dragons, right?"

"The others, maybe, but not me. Tell Parker I'm working."

Etta didn't look impressed. "You can't continue hiding in here. You're going to have to talk to him eventually, and the sooner you do it, the better."

"I don't have time to talk to him." Ansley sounded like a spoiled child, but he didn't care. The thought of talking to Parker sent him into a panic.

He still didn't know how to reconcile Parker with Byron. If Parker had still been Byron, it would have been fairly easy for Ansley to get used to having him in his life again. Everything would have gone back to the way it had been before. Eventually, he'd have wrapped his mind around everything being the way it had been before.

But there was no Byron anymore. There was Parker, and Ansley didn't know what to do with the man. It was like the world was giving him a second chance, or rather, like it was dangling a new, improved Byron in front of him, and at the same time, telling him that he couldn't have the man he'd been in love with for a hundred or so years. What was he supposed to do with this? How was he supposed to accept that even though he finally had his dragon back, things had changed?

Etta grinned. "Well, whether you want it or not, I'm letting him in. Hopefully, you'll finally stop snapping at people once this is over."

She vanished before Ansley could tell her not to let Parker in. They were all plotting to get him to talk to Parker, and this was only the first step. If he didn't give in, it would escalate, and if Penley got involved, it would turn into a disaster. Maybe Etta was right, and Ansley should talk to Parker now. They could get things out of the way, and Ansley would reassure Parker that he didn't owe him anything.

"Ansley?" Parker's voice called out from just outside the door.

Ansley sucked in a breath. He could do this. He could be an adult and ignore his feelings for the next ten minutes. He could answer Parker's questions and reassure him, wait to break down until Parker was gone.

He had to.

"Come in."

Parker did, looking hesitant. Ansley plastered a smile on his face because he didn't want Parker to feel like he wasn't welcome, even though Ansley had no idea what to do with him. This was Parker's home, no matter how Ansley felt about him or the entire situation. Ansley would do everything he could to make him feel that way, and he'd do it with a smile on his face. Whether that smile was real or not was another matter entirely, one that wasn't Parker's business.

"Hi," Parker said as he closed the door.

"I wasn't aware you wanted to talk to me. I would have made myself available if I'd known."

Parker stared at Ansley for a moment before snorting. "That's bullshit."

Ansley's eyes widened. "Excuse me?"

"I don't think I have to repeat myself, but I will since you're having trouble processing my words. That's bullshit."

Ansley wanted Parker to leave. He almost told him to, but he felt he owed to have at least this conversation. "I've been working. I'm sure that by now, you're aware that everyone here wants to find their dragon, and I'm the only one who can do it. You're not the center of the universe. You're here, but you're only one of six."

Parker raised his hands. "I apologize, and I do understand that. But we both know you've been working so much because you're hiding from me, and I don't like being lied to."

Ansley glared. "I'm not lying. I've been working, and the sooner I do this, the sooner we'll get the other dragons back. Besides, I thought you'd have enough to distract yourself. You can explore the castle, talk to the others, and spend time with Matthias."

Parker sighed. "Can I sit down?"

Ansley wanted to say no, but he doubted it would go over well. "If you really have to, but I have more work to do."

Parker stared. "I'm not surprised. I'll be as quick as I can."

Ansley nodded and settled back in his chair. He watched as Parker sat on the other side of his desk, facing him. His heart raced as he wondered what was about to happen.

Parker didn't mince his words. He seemed like the kind of guy who went straight to the point, and Ansley didn't know how to deal with that. Byron had been that way, too, but he'd been brutal about it. He'd never hesitated to tell Ansley how he felt and what he thought of him, and more often than not, it had been hurtful.

Maybe Parker wasn't that different from Byron after all.

Parker didn't know where to start. He wanted to smooth things out between him and Ansley, but it was clear that Ansley was almost afraid of him for some reason. He didn't want to talk to Parker, and he'd been avoiding him, no matter what he said about working. That made Parker wonder even more about what kind of person he'd been before. Ansley didn't know him as Parker, which meant that the reason he was avoiding him was Byron.

There was nothing Parker could do to change the past, but he wasn't Byron anymore. He hadn't been for a hundred years, and he needed Ansley to understand that. Whatever had happened between them before, it wouldn't happen again.

Or at least, Parker hoped so.

He didn't want Ansley to be wary or afraid of him. He didn't want the mage to keep his distance and reach out only when he needed to be protected. It didn't sit right with him that Ansley was afraid when he was supposed to be protecting him.

Going straight to personal questions wouldn't be good. Ansley was wary as it was, and it would be even worse if Parker asked him why he was that way. So Parker decided to stay professional. Besides, he needed his questions answered. "I've been here a few days now, and I'd like to know what you expect from me," he said.

Ansley blinked, his expression telling Parker he hadn't expected that question. "What do you mean?"

"Well, I'm your dragon. I know it means I'm supposed to protect you, but I'm not sure what or how to do that. I have no doubt that Byron knew what he was doing, but I'm not him, and I wouldn't be able to fight my way out of a wet paper

93

bag."

Ansley's eyes had stayed wide. He stared at Parker as if he didn't recognize him, and Parker realized that maybe Ansley had expected things to go back to the way they'd been before. He knew a version of Parker that didn't exist, and clearly, he hadn't realized that Parker was different. Maybe he would have if he'd spent time with Parker, but if Byron had been as awful as Parker suspected, it would make sense that Ansley hadn't wanted to.

Dammit. Parker hated his old self, even though he couldn't remember him.

Ansley cleared his throat. "You're right. Byron was a great fighter. He'd been raised as one in his clan, and it was a surprise to no one when he ended up being a mage's shield. The clan viewed that position as a great honor. They still do."

Parker licked his lips. He had questions about his past, but he was afraid to ask. "The clan still exists, then?"

Ansley's expression did a complicated thing Parker couldn't read. "They do. I can put you in contact with them if you want. Initially, they called me every month to find out if I had information about you, but over the past few decades, they stopped. I'm sure they gave up hope I'd find you again. I don't blame them, either. It took me way too long."

"But you've been doing everything you could for a hundred years."

"Clearly, everything I could do wasn't enough."

It was almost as if he expected Parker to agree with him, but he didn't. He had no idea what went into the spell Ansley had cast to find him, but he had no doubt it was complicated and not something most people would be able to do. Maybe it was good that the clan had stayed away after a while. "Maybe I'll contact them eventually. For now, I'd like to settle down, which is why I'm here. What do you expect me to do?"

"Just to get used to living here. This is your home now."

"I can do that during my free time. I'm used to working, and even though I don't know where to start, I take my job as your protector seriously."

Ansley shrugged. "That's nice to hear, but there's nothing to protect me from."

"What did Byron do when he wasn't protecting you, then?" Parker was getting frustrated but didn't want to snap at Ansley. The mage already feared him enough.

"The usual. He trained, visited his clan, and spent time with the other shields. We didn't really spend much time together unless he was working."

"Is that why you stayed away? Because you thought I wouldn't want to spend time with you?"

"I don't see why it would have changed. Byron always told me to stay away from him unless I needed him, and that's what I've been doing. You don't have to worry about me. Even if there was something to protect me from, I'm safe at the castle. You can do whatever you want. We have an extensive library, and the area is empty of humans, so you can fly and stretch your wings. If you don't feel comfortable doing that, I can cast a spell that'll make you invisible to humans. You can explore the area and the castle."

Parker was looking forward to that, but it didn't answer the question he was here to ask. "My job is to protect you. I need to be able to do that."

"Then you could train. I'm sure Tyne would be happy to show you a few tips. Again, though, I don't believe it's necessary. There's no danger at the moment."

Ansley made it sound like Parker didn't have a reason to be here, but Parker didn't believe it. "What did I protect you from back then?"

"Other mages, mostly, but not just that. People used to reach out to us when they needed help of the magical kind. You came with me and made sure they didn't hurt me."

"So that's what I'm supposed to do now?"

Ansley shook his head. "We haven't accepted jobs from anyone since we lost our shields. It would have left us unprotected, and we don't need the money. We lost many contacts since then because of that, so you don't have to worry. People haven't reached out for help in a long time."

It sounded like Ansley was upset that he wasn't helping anymore, which Parker could understand. If Ansley's job had been to help people and he'd had to stop because he lost his shield, he had to have been sorry. Maybe he'd hoped that with Byron back, he'd be able to start again, but instead, he was stuck with Parker. Parker didn't blame him for being disappointed.

He wanted to keep Ansley safe, but he realized it wouldn't be easy because he had no clue what to do. Having Ansley stay at the castle was the best way to do that, but it made Parker feel guilty. Ansley had been stuck here for long enough. Now that he had his shield back, he was supposed to be free and to be able to help people like he had before. He was supposed to be protected. The only reason he wasn't was that Parker had lost his memories.

"You think there's a way to get my memories back?"

"I don't know. I'm not an expert on memory spells, and we're still not sure what Carlyle did. He managed to somehow take all your memories and spirit you away from us simultaneously. Do you know how much power he has to have used to do that? He moved six dragon shifters, six shields that were magically linked to their mages. He made you impossible to find for decades. Honestly, I'd strangle him if I could get my hands on him again."

Parker grinned. "Don't tempt me."

With Ansley smiling back at him, it felt like everything would be all right. Then Ansley's smile vanished, and he turned serious again. "I wouldn't worry too much if I were you. I'm not going anywhere until we find another dragon, so you don't have to worry about protecting me from anything. I'm perfectly safe here at the castle. We have wards everywhere to make sure no one can come in if we don't want them to. Focus on your new life, not on me."

The problem was that it didn't sit right with Parker. He was here for a reason, and that reason wasn't himself. It was Ansley, and he needed to make things right with the mage.

Ansley wouldn't have taken pity on Byron, but the same couldn't be said for Parker. He looked so confused and lost that Ansley couldn't help but reach out. After all, he knew how feeling lost felt like. He'd been that way since he lost Byron, and the only thing that had helped had been to focus on the spell to find the dragons again.

Parker's place was with them. Even though there was no danger to Ansley, it hadn't always been that way. Dragons and mages traveled together, helped the magical and supernatural community, and worked as a team. They hadn't done that for far too long, but things were changing. Ansley had to focus on finding the other dragons, but they could open up once he had. They could finally leave the protection of the castle for longer stretches of time, and they could start helping people again.

He couldn't wait.

He wanted to reassure Parker that he was perfectly fine doing whatever he wanted. It wouldn't help to get Parker to train when he had no idea what he was doing. Tyne could help since he'd kept up his training for the past hundred years, but he wasn't a dragon. Hopefully, some of the others would remember. If they didn't, they'd have to reach out to the clans, and Ansley wasn't sure it was a good idea. He didn't remember Byron's clan with fondness.

"Look," he said, trying to find a way to make Parker feel better. "You should check the library. We have many books, and a lot of them are on dragons, mages, and their bond. They'll help you understand, and maybe you can start from there and continue learning. You should also spend time with your boyfriend. You dragged him here for a reason, right?"

Parker frowned. "Please tell me you're not talking about Matthias."

"He's the one person you wanted to bring home with you."

"Because he's my best friend, and I didn't want to do this on my own. We've never been together, though."

Ansley told himself not to betray how he was feeling. "Why not?"

"Have you ever been with any of the other mages?"

Ansley shuddered at the thought. "Of course not. They're my brothers, even though we're not related."

"The same goes for Matthias and me. We've never been anything but friends, and that's not going to change."

Ansley told himself that didn't mean Parker wanted him. He hadn't wanted him when he was Byron, and Ansley doubted that had changed.

"But I'm glad I didn't have to leave him behind," Parker continued. "I always tried to keep people away because I had to move every ten years or so, and it was easier if I didn't have to leave friends behind. Matthias wouldn't take no for an answer, though, and I was dreading having to go. I was about to do just that when you appeared in my life. I was afraid to tell him I could turn into a dragon and that I wasn't aging, but he took it much better than I thought. He even agreed to come with me, and it's nice to have a familiar face, even though you and the other mages are nice. All of this is almost like a dream, you know? I don't remember any of it, but I wish I could."

Ansley was glad Parker didn't remember being Byron, even though it would have helped both of them come to terms with what was happening. It would have made their lives easier, but knowing how annoying Byron found him, Ansley decided he liked Parker much better.

It had nothing to do with the fact that since Matthias wasn't Parker's boyfriend, Ansley might have a chance with him.

Ansley realized he'd been selfish. It didn't matter if Parker was with Matthias or if he never wanted Ansley. Parker was where he belonged, a place he never should have been taken from. Now that he was back, he could have a home and a family, and even if he never remembered being Byron, his life would be more complete. It would take time to work things out, especially as they continued finding the other dragons, but Ansley needed Parker to be happy. Parker was his dragon, and while Parker's job was to protect Ansley, Ansley had a specific responsibility toward him. He should protect Parker, and he would, even if it wasn't the same way Parker could protect him. He didn't have fangs and claws, and he didn't have anything or anyone to protect Parker from, but they were a team. They had to work as one, and hiding from Parker in the fear that he'd become Byron again wouldn't help either of them.

Ansley might get hurt, but he also might not. Parker wasn't the same person Byron had been, and whether or not he got his memories back, he was here now. It was Ansley's duty to stand next to him and keep him happy, and he would, even if it hurt.

He forced himself to smile. "I understand you're lost and confused, and I am, too. It'll take us some time to find a way to work together, but I have faith in our bond. For now, you don't have to protect me because I'm safe. Use that time to go over the books we have in the library and find your bearings. We can talk again in a few days, or maybe a few weeks."

"What will happen if you find another dragon?"

"I'll come to you and tell you. I won't go alone, I promise."

That seemed to satisfy Parker, who nodded. "Good. I'm pretty sure my dragon wouldn't allow you to leave without me. Maybe I should shift and find out if I can protect you in that form."

"I have no doubt you can. Your dragon is fierce, and if you want to shift, feel free to do it. You're safe here, Parker. You don't have to hide who and what you are anymore."

The smile Parker gave Ansley was worth any pain Ansley might feel in the future.

CHAPTER EIGHT

"You're still avoiding him."

Ansley groaned and looked up from the map he'd been bent over. He wasn't surprised to find Jarvis at his office door, but it didn't mean he was happy. "I'm not avoiding him."

Jarvis arched a brow and stepped in. "Is that why you still aren't taking your meals with us?"

"No, I'm not eating with you because I'm working on finding the other shields." Ansley pushed away the map and leaned back in his chair. "Do you know how frustrating it is? The spell worked once, which means it should work again, yet it doesn't. I tried using a world map, but it still didn't find anything. I focused on Marlow, but nothing."

Jarvis walked around Ansley's desk and sat on the edge of it. He squeezed Ansley's shoulder, and Ansley closed his eyes and allowed the presence of the man he considered a big brother to soothe him.

He didn't know what to do. He'd tried everything he could think of, yet he still hadn't found Marlow. He wanted to give the dragon back to Jarvis, but he'd failed and felt incredibly guilty about it.

Why was he the only one who had his dragon back when his relationship with Byron had been so bad? He should have looked for Marlow first, but Jarvis had insisted he needed to find his own dragon. Maybe Jarvis had been right, but it didn't explain why Ansley was having so much trouble finding Marlow. He'd even tried finding another dragon, but the result had been the same.

Nothing.

"You're working too much," Jarvis said. "Exhausting yourself isn't going to help."

"Maybe it will. At this point, I don't know what else I can do."

"How about you spend some time with your dragon? Parker has been hanging around the castle, looking like a lost puppy. I'm sure he could use your help."

"We already talked about it, and we agreed he didn't need to protect me as long as I'm in the castle. I told him to poke around the library and stretch his wings." And spend more time with Matthias, but Ansley didn't want to think about that.

Parker had told him he and Matthias were only friends and that it wouldn't change, and maybe that was true. Ansley wasn't jealous of Matthias anymore, but even if he and Parker weren't together, it didn't change anything for Ansley. Mages and dragons usually ended up together, but not always, and clearly, not in Ansley's case. The fact that Parker had lost his Byron memories wouldn't change that.

"He's been doing that, but I feel the two of you should spend time together. Penley's been looking into getting Parker's memories back, but so far, he hit a wall. He spent time with Parker, and he says it's like the memories have never been there at all. They were taken from him, not shielded or hidden."

"And you can't get back what's not there anymore."

"Exactly. I doubt anything we can do will get Parker's memories back."

Ansley shouldn't be happy about that. He should want Parker to feel complete, especially since not being able to remember how to defend the castle and protect Ansley and the other mages clearly frustrated him. "So it should be fine for me to continue working."

"I'm not telling you not to work. I know nothing I can do or say will take you away from your desk, and that's fine. But we've been looking for the dragons for decades, and you have yours back. Eventually, after you find the others, we'll be able to return to a normal life, which means you'll have to spend more time with Parker. You should start now that we're still in the castle."

"I will once I find a way to make the spell work again."

Jarvis looked disappointed. "He's not Byron anymore."

Ansley looked away. "I'm aware of that."

"Are you? Because I could understand you staying away from Byron, considering the way he treated you, but not from Parker. I was wary initially, but he's such a different man that it's hard to believe. We talked about what happened to him after he woke up in the forest, and being alone, having to work for everything he had, turned him into another man. If he remembered anything from the time he was Byron, he'd be horrified."

"I'm aware of all of that. I'm not sure why you're telling me."

"Because you need to stop behaving as if Parker is Byron. You need to give him a chance." He hesitated. "Maybe this time, there's a possibility that the two of you will end up together. You've always been in love with him, but it was a bad idea for you to feel that way when he was Byron. I can't say the same for Parker."

Ansley was already shaking his head. "I'm not in love with him."

"You're right. You're in love with Byron, and Parker isn't Byron. You need to give Parker a chance, though. At the very least, you have to be able to work with him."

He wasn't wrong. No matter how much Ansley tried to ignore it, once they had all the dragons back, they could go back to the life they'd had before. That meant Ansley would need to be comfortable with Parker, and while he still couldn't allow himself to hope something could happen between them, he needed to let Parker in. It was great that Parker was spending time with the other mages, but Ansley was his mage. He needed to stop rejecting Parker and hiding in his office.

He sighed and thumped the back of his head against his chair. "Fine. I'll put my work aside for meals."

Jarvis beamed as if Ansley had offered him the world. "That's all I ask for. We miss you, and we've been worried you're working too much."

"I probably am, but this spell is driving me nuts."

"Maybe taking a step away will help you see it more clearly. It worked before, which means it has to work again. You're missing something, and obsessing over it clearly isn't helping. Put everything away for a while and come downstairs to have dinner with us."

Ansley couldn't say no. He missed spending time with his brothers and needed to stop avoiding Parker. Besides, maybe Jarvis was right and stepping away from the spell would give him enough space to identify what he was missing.

Because he *was* missing something, and as soon as he understood what it was, he'd be able to cast the spell again and find Marlow.

Parker wasn't used to living with so many people. During the day, he could deal with it because most of the mages were busy. Even at lunch, they preferred eating in their office or wherever they were working.

Dinner was different.

At dinner, they all gathered in the massive dining room. Well, all except Ansley. Parker had yet to see him during meals, and even though Ansley had reassured him that it was because he was working, he couldn't help but wonder if there was more behind it. Could the mage still be avoiding Parker? He'd given Parker tips as to what to do, but the library was intimidating. There were so many books that Parker didn't know where to start, which meant he was going to need help. He would have gone back to Ansley, but he was afraid of pushing the man away. Ansley already seemed so wary of him. Would Parker pushing back into his life make things worse?

But if Parker kept his distance, could they build a relationship? Parker wasn't an idiot. He was aware that Ansley had hidden many things from him about when he'd been Byron. He'd limited himself to explaining that he and Byron had worked together but that it hadn't been for long. Parker had gotten the impression that he'd been an asshole as Byron, and it didn't sit right with him. If he'd hurt Ansley, he wanted to fix it, but he didn't know if he could. Would Ansley allow him to?

"You need to taste this," Matthias said, dropping a spoonful of what looked like mashed potatoes on Parker's plate. "It's delicious. I need to know who cooked it," he told the table.

All the mages were there except for Jarvis and Ansley. No one seemed surprised that Ansley wasn't present, but Jarvis was usually at dinner with them. Parker wondered why he wasn't tonight. Maybe he had something to do?

"Jillian takes good care of us," Dallin explained. "She's the best cook we've had in decades."

"She's a woman?" Matthias wrinkled his nose. "Dammit. I wanted to marry her."

Dallin laughed. "I suppose you still can."

"Yes, but I'm not into women that way. I might change that for these mashed potatoes, though."

Tyne grunted from his chair next to Dallin, but he didn't point out how ridiculous Matthias was being. Matthias was human, and Parker had been afraid that the mages might treat him differently, but everyone had been welcoming so far. Matthias wasn't the only human who lived in the castle. Everyone but the mages was human, from the cook to the housekeepers to the assistants who helped the mages with their work. Parker had asked Penley why none of the mages seemed to have apprentices, but the question had made Penley so uncomfortable that Parker hadn't pushed when he hadn't explained. It had made him curious, though.

"We've all wanted to marry Jillian at one time or another," Jarvis said as he walked in.

Parker looked up, a smile already on his face, to greet the mage. His eyes widened when he saw who was behind him. He wasn't the only one surprised, either. Tyne grunted while Keylon beamed.

"What did you have to promise him to get him here?" he asked Jarvis.

Ansley glared at him, his focus on the food on the table. "Jillian's food is enough to get me to dinner."

Ansley plopped into one of the empty chairs, his hands already reaching for the food. Parker couldn't look away. He was glad to see Ansley. Hopefully, his presence tonight meant he was done avoiding Parker.

He looked around the table. It was hard for him to wrap his mind around the fact that all these people had known him before. Most of them had fallen back into a strange familiarity he couldn't make sense of, although he supposed that was because he didn't have memories of them. They treated him like a long-lost friend, which he was. It would be easier if he could remember them, but sometimes, when things hinted at the fact that he'd been an asshole when he was Byron, he was glad he couldn't.

He didn't want to be a dick. He didn't want Ansley to avoid him just because of the past and how he'd been back then. He needed the mages, especially Ansley, to understand that he wasn't the same man anymore. He wasn't sure how to make that happen, but he'd find a way.

He wasn't going to lose the family he'd just found because of mistakes he couldn't remember making.

"Everything okay?" Matthias asked, leaning closer to Parker.

Parker smiled at him. He didn't want Matthias to be worried. There was no reason for him to be, and there was nothing he could do to change the situation. "I'm fine."

"You're sure? Because you don't look fine. You look a bit confused and lost, to be honest."

Parker looked around the table again. Tyne was focused on his food while Penley was gently teasing Ansley. Jarvis looked at them with a smile on his lips, almost like a proud father, even though he wasn't that much older than them.

"It's weird," Parker whispered. "They remember me, and they treat me like a friend. I don't remember them, though."

"I don't think it matters. They love you and don't care that you're not the same person you were before."

Parker snorted. "I'm pretty sure that at least a few of them are happy I'm not the person I was before."

"Yeah, I got the impression that you weren't very nice, at least to Ansley, which I don't understand. He's sweet and cute, and when you're not looking, he stares at you as if you hung the moon. Were you two an item before?"

"Nope. He made sure I knew we weren't."

"Uh. I got the impression that it was expected, but maybe it's because you hadn't known him long before this mess happened."

"About a year," Parker explained.

"Then maybe you didn't have the opportunity to explore what could have been between you. Or maybe you really were such a dick that Ansley stayed away from you. I'm pretty sure he has a crush on you, though, and you're a nice guy now."

Parker liked to think that might be true, but everything in this situation was confusing as hell. "I wish I could talk to another shield. Maybe they'd be able to tell me if I'm missing something."

"I guess it would be easier for you if you had someone to talk to, but the other shields probably don't have any more memories than you do. I'm afraid that even when the mages find them, you'll all be running around in the dark, trying to make sense of everything."

And wasn't that the truth. Parker hoped that having a dragon nearby would help, though. Maybe they could make sense of things together rather than having him do all this by himself. Even if no other dragon knew what they were doing, it would be easier to figure things out as a group rather than alone.

Or at least, he hoped so.

Matthias patted Parker's hand. "Now stop worrying so much and eat your mashed potatoes. I'll eat them for you if you don't."

Parker leaned over his plate and wrapped an arm around it as he pulled it closer while glaring at Matthias. "Don't you dare."

Matthias laughed, and Parker reminded himself that whatever happened next, he'd never lose his best friend. He hoped to be able to make things right with Ansley, but even if he couldn't, he knew who he was now, or rather, who he'd been. He'd wondered for decades about that and about the people he'd left behind, and now, he had answers. They might not be the ones he'd been hoping for, but he was starting to realize that his past didn't matter and that it never had. He wasn't Byron anymore, and even if he got his memories back, he never would be again. He was Parker, and he had the opportunity of showing the people around him that he was a good person and that he deserved to have them in his life.

He had every intention of doing just that.

Dinner had been good, like Ansley had known it would be. He'd tried so hard to stay away from everyone since he and Jarvis had come back with Parker that he'd almost forgotten how nice it was to be surrounded by his brothers. He still needed to focus on his work, but it was good to have an evening off and stop obsessing over finding the other dragons and the stone where Carlyle was trapped.

But now dinner was over, and even though it was getting late, Ansley wanted to go back to his office. He was still tinkering with the spell, trying to find a way to make it work again, and he was getting antsy not being able to. So he took advantage of dessert being served to sneak out of the dining room. No one noticed him, not even Jarvis, who was bickering with Penley over which dessert was best, ice cream or tiramisu.

As far as Ansley was concerned, chocolate won every time, in whatever form it was.

"Hey, can I talk to you for a moment?"

The voice behind Ansley made him freeze. He was still in the hallway outside the dining room, and he'd thought he could get away without anyone stopping him. His brothers hadn't seen him sneak out, or maybe they had and ignored it, but not Matthias.

Ansley sucked in a breath. He reminded himself that Matthias was Parker's best friend and that he was here because he cared about Parker. Ansley did, too, even though he didn't understand why. Part of it was the bond, of course, but he'd been keeping his distance from Parker on purpose. He didn't want to care about him as much as he'd cared about Byron.

That way lay pain, and he wasn't ready to put his heart through that again.

Still, he plastered a smile on his lips and turned to face Matthias. "What can I do for you?"

Matthias stared at him, making Ansley want to run. Instead, he shuffled his feet, trying to look at ease, knowing he wasn't succeeding.

"I just wanted to say thank you," Matthias eventually said.

Ansley had no idea what he was talking about. "What?"

"For what you've done. You didn't have to bring me along, and eventually, you'd have convinced Parker to leave me behind. But you didn't even try. You allowed me to come, even though this isn't my place. I don't belong here the way Parker does, but I'm glad for the opportunity you and the other mages have given me. I never imagined such a world existed or that my best friend could turn into a big ass dragon. Which I still haven't seen, by the way. I've been trying to convince Parker to show me, but I think he's afraid I'll faint or something like that. He thinks I'll be terrified of him, and I might be if it wasn't Parker we're talking about, you know?"

Ansley had no idea what to do with the word vomit that had just come out of Matthias's mouth. Should he nod and go along with it? No matter what Matthias was to Parker, he'd always be part of Parker's life. Ansley was convinced of that, which meant that if he wanted to keep Parker in his life, he'd need to deal with Matthias. Clearly, Matthias was trying to reach out to him, and while Ansley doubted they'd ever become friends, they could be friendly, at the very least. It was a requirement if they'd both be in Parker's life.

So Ansley smiled again, trying to make it more natural this time around. He didn't want Matthias to think he didn't like him. He didn't know the other man enough to like or dislike him. "There's nothing to thank me for. Parker asked if you could come, and Jarvis and I both agreed it would be best, considering his memory loss. You're the only person he knows, and we didn't want him to lose that."

"But he knows you, too."

"Part of him does. He doesn't recognize me, though, and I don't blame him. I hate that his memories were taken from him, and we're trying to change that, but I'm afraid it's not looking good. He needs you here, which is why we were more than happy to welcome you to the castle."

"Most people would have said no and kicked me out," Matthias pointed out.

"Then I suppose we're not most people. Besides, you're hardly the only human who lives with us."

"About that. How did you find all these people? How did you convince them not to say anything about what you are?"

"We didn't have to ask. Most of them have been with us for decades, and in some cases, like Jillian, they grew up here. Her mother was our cook before her. She's known about us all her life and loves us like brothers."

"It has to be strange for her to see you stay young while she gets older."

"It doesn't have to be that way. Dragons stay young because of their innate magic, but the same doesn't go for mages. We have to use spells, and we offer the same spells to all the humans we trust and who have been working with us for so long. We've been keeping Jillian the way she is now for a few years. Thorne has always said no, but I think he's going to cave eventually."

Matthias's eyes went wide. "You mean that I could stay young, too? I could stay like this and be with Parker for decades?"

Ansley wanted Parker to have everything he wished for, including Matthias by his side for hundreds of years. It shouldn't hurt as much as it did, especially since Parker had explained that he and Matthias had only ever been friends, but Ansley couldn't help but wonder if that might change. Parker didn't have to hide such a massive part of his life from Matthias anymore. He could be himself, and maybe, it would lead to more. What would Ansley do if it did? Could he watch them fall in love and be together for decades to come?

He already knew the answer to that. "We can do that, sure," he told Matthias. "Everything's a bit of a mess, but if you're bent on staying this age, we can do it."

"Oh, I'm fine aging a little bit more. Honestly, I just found out about this, so I'd like to think about it. It's good to know I have the option, though. I didn't want Parker to lose me." He hesitated. "You know, you should give him a chance."

"He's my shield."

Matthias shook his head. "Not that way. You've been pushing him away, which I understand. It has to be a mess for you to have him back in your life after so long, especially since he can't remember you. What I meant is that you should give him a chance to show you he can care about you. I know that you and Parker weren't together back when he was Byron, and honestly, from what little I've heard, it makes sense because he was an asshole. I'm having a hard time imagining Parker that way, but he's had a hundred years to change, so I don't see him as Byron. I realize it has to be harder for you, but please, allow him to show you he's not the same person anymore. I've been told that dragons and shields usually end up together, and I guess it makes sense. He's been beating himself up for treating you badly when he was Byron, and yes, he's completely lost and has no idea how to be a shield, but maybe give him a chance?"

Ansley understood what Matthias was saying. He'd known all of it except for the fact that Matthias thought Parker cared about him. He didn't understand how that could be, since they'd barely talked, but he couldn't deny it was his fault. He'd only been thinking about himself, and it was selfish. He'd been protecting his heart, keeping Parker away because he was afraid of getting hurt, and he hadn't considered how Parker had to feel.

Of course he was lost. Of course he had no idea how to be a shield. Ansley was the one person who should be explaining things to him and helping him through this, but instead, he'd been hiding.

He wanted Parker to feel at home here at the castle, to feel like he belonged. He deserved it after being away for so long. "I'll give him a chance," he told Matthias.

He'd have thought he'd handed Matthias the moon from his wide smile. "Good. You won't regret it."

Ansley hoped he wouldn't. He also hoped he wouldn't lose his heart to Parker the way he'd lost it to Byron, but what were the chances of that not happening?

CHAPTER NINE

Ansley jerked up into a sitting position. The wave of magic rolled over his skin, giving him goosebumps. He ignored the sensation, scrambling out of his bed and looking around wildly. Where had the magic come from? Was it one of the wards?

He sucked in a breath and told himself to calm down. Panicking wouldn't help anyone, and it wouldn't solve whatever this was. He needed to know what had happened, and he wouldn't find out if he kept freaking out.

He grabbed the massive hoodie he wore in his rooms, pulled it over his head, stuffed his feet into his slippers, and rushed out of his bedroom.

He wasn't the only one. Tyne was already in the hallway when Ansley barged out of his room, looking like he was about to kill someone. He only wore a pair of tight boxer briefs, which normally would have flustered Ansley. This time, he ignored it.

"What was it?" he asked.

Tyne shook his head. "I don't know."

The others started coming out of their rooms, too. Penley wore a pair of pajama pants with Christmas trees stamped on them, along with a black t-shirt with three gnomes on it. The writing said *Chilling with my gnomies*, which would have made Ansley smile in any other circumstance. Penley looked frightened, though, and he wasn't the only one.

Jarvis appeared, wearing a fluffy pale blue robe. "It can't be," he said, looking at the others.

Ansley didn't want to think about what this could mean. "Only a few mages could create a wave of magic so strong that we felt it the way we did."

"I agree, but he's trapped."

"He *was*. What if he's not anymore?" What if what they'd felt was Carlyle getting out of the stone?

There was a reason they'd been looking for the stone for so long. They should have killed Carlyle, considering how dangerous he was, but while Tyne had been all for that plan, Jarvis's heart was soft, and he hadn't been able to kill his apprentice. They'd agreed to trap him in the stone so they could always keep an eye on him, and while they'd managed to do just that, Carlyle hadn't gone without a fight. On his way out, he'd cast the spell that had torn the dragons from the mages. It had knocked the mages unconscious, and the stone was gone by the time they'd woken up. They'd been looking for it since then, with no clues as to where it was. They had no idea who had it, but over the years, they'd relaxed. Whoever had the stone, Carlyle had been stuck in it.

But possibly not anymore.

Ansley ran down the hallway, knowing what he had to do. He could feel and hear the others behind him, but he ignored them. They needed answers, and there was only one way to find out if Carlyle was free.

Ansley had been casting a seeking spell every so often since they'd trapped Carlyle, but it had always come up empty. He hoped the same would happen now as he quickly spread a map on his desk, focused on it, and tried to find Carlyle. He didn't have any of the candles and herbs he usually used, but he didn't need them to focus this time. When he reached for the magic, it answered easily, confused and scared. It gave him what he needed. The scorched sign on the map when he opened his eyes was proof of that.

Keylon sucked in a breath. "It can't be."

"I don't want to believe it, but this is proof. He's back. He somehow managed to get out of the stone," Ansley told the other mages who'd gathered around his desk.

Jarvis was pale. "What do we do? We only have one shield, and we can't face Carlyle like this. He's too strong."

"Maybe the decades trapped in the stone will have made him weaker," Ansley said, desperately trying to find a way to reassure both himself and the others.

This was a disaster. Back when they'd trapped Carlyle, it had taken all their dragons' magic and support to make it happen. It was true that Carlyle had been trapped for a hundred years, and in that time, they'd all been busy studying and strengthening their magic, but they'd done so without their dragons. Even worse, the dragons had no memories, which meant that even if they found them, they wouldn't be able to help the way they should. It would be way too easy for Carlyle to take them on and win this time, which wasn't something Ansley wanted to consider.

But what could they do? They couldn't face Carlyle like this. They needed more dragons, and Ansley was the only one who could find them.

"We have to go there," Tyne said, tilting his chin at the map.

"We can't," Jarvis told him. "We don't have our dragons."

"But one of us does." Tyne looked at Ansley. "We can't know if Carlyle is free or if it's just someone trying to get him out. We won't find out unless one of us goes there, and you're the only one who can do that."

"But Parker doesn't know what to do. He might be my shield, but he doesn't know how to protect me." And Ansley wasn't about to put Parker in danger.

But it was true that they needed to find out what had happened. He'd found Carlyle on the map, but it might just be because whoever had the stone was trying to get him out of it. If this person had managed to break through some of the wards they'd put on the stone, it might make Carlyle's presence in the human world more obvious to magic, but it didn't mean he was out.

There wasn't much they could do without knowing what was happening. That meant Ansley and Parker would have to go to the spot on the map and poke around. Hopefully, they'd find the stone and secure it. Ansley didn't want to think about what would happen if Carlyle had been freed.

That was the worst-case scenario, especially since they didn't have the other dragons yet. Ansley couldn't think about that, though. He had to focus on what they *did* have and what they *could* do.

Even though it wasn't enough.

Parker didn't think any of the mages had noticed him. He'd been woken up by a wave of something he hadn't recognized, at least not in his human brain. His dragon had known, though, and he'd helpfully informed Parker that it was a wave of magic. Parker had decided that couldn't be a good thing, which was why he'd left his bedroom.

He was right.

He'd found the mages rushing away and followed them to Ansley's office. Ansley had been focused on a map, and all the mages had been staring at it, especially after a burned spot had appeared. Parker had been impressed until he realized the mages had no idea what was happening. They were afraid, and from what little Parker had been told about this Carlyle guy, they were right to be.

He understood. The last time the mages had faced Carlyle, they'd been powerful and had their dragons with them. Parker might not fully understand how magic between mages and dragons worked, but he'd been told that the bond between a mage and a dragon meant that the mage could use powerful magic they normally wouldn't be able to control. If that was how they'd trapped Carlyle, how were they supposed to do it now? They only had one dragon, and Parker couldn't remember anything of that time of his life. He couldn't help them, and he hated it.

There was nothing he could do, hanging around Ansley's office. The mages needed to talk, and Parker needed to do something to help. So he headed to the library, hoping once again he'd find a book that would explain to him what he was supposed to do.

He'd been poking around for days now. Many of the books he'd found had explained the bond between dragon and mage and the role a dragon had in a mage's life, but he was starting to think that he needed a more hands-on explanation. If he had to learn how to fight, it wouldn't do him any good to try doing so by reading a book.

But it was the middle of the night, and there was nothing else he could do. He doubted he'd be able to go back to sleep, and the library was the next best thing.

He turned the lights on once he got there and looked around. There was a truly impressive number of books, and it had scared him when he'd first walked in. It still did, especially because he didn't know if there were answers to his questions here. The only way to find out was to poke around more books, and he decided to try a new area. So far, none of the books he'd found had helped. Maybe he needed to move to another shelf.

He grabbed a few books from several shelves, then went to sit in one of the armchairs by the massive fireplace. There was no fire burning, but it was still comforting, especially with the blanket Parker found on the back of the armchair. It was clear someone spent a lot of time here, and he hoped that whichever mage it was wouldn't mind him borrowing it.

He flipped through the first book, but it was focused on the history of magic, and while it was interesting, it wasn't what he needed. The next book held more promise, and he started reading about the bond between mages and dragons.

The book explained that once a mage and a dragon worked together, they could exchange magic. Dragons were massive, and their shift happened because of magic, which meant they held a vast amount of it. Some mages had apparently tried using dragons without their consent, and it hadn't ended well. There had been a war a long time ago between mages and dragons, but thankfully, it had ended, and dragons had agreed to offer their people when the magic chose a specific mage for them and if the dragon agreed to it.

Parker leaned his head back and stared at the ceiling. He'd already known the magic had chosen him for Ansley, and since they'd spent a year together back then, it meant he'd agreed to become Ansley's dragon. Why had he done so since he'd clearly disliked Ansley? What would have happened if he'd said no? Would the magic have given Ansley another dragon? Did every mage have a dragon?

He turned his attention back to the book, frowning as he read. The author had a flowery way of talking about the bond, and it was clear that whoever had written the book was fully on board with the mage and dragon being in a relationship. A few things caught Parker's attention.

The author believed the bond became stronger after the dragon and mage were united physically. It could happen through a spell, too, but the author clearly disliked that option. They seemed to believe that a bond consolidated through a spell wouldn't be as strong and secure and could be broken much more easily.

Was that what had happened? Clearly, the author thought that sex was the best way for a mage and a dragon to bond. Considering what he knew about Byron, Parker doubted his old self would have agreed to do that with Ansley. Did that mean that his bond with Ansley wasn't as strong as the bond between, say, Jarvis and Marlow? And why hadn't anyone told him this before? He would have thought Ansley would have at least mentioned it, although maybe not. Ansley had taken great care to stay away from him, as if he was afraid of how he'd react if he found out about this. Maybe that was what had happened. Maybe Ansley hadn't told Parker about the sex thing because he thought Parker would believe he was expected to do it.

What did all of this mean? That Parker and Ansley needed to have sex? Parker wasn't Byron, and he couldn't say he'd mind having to sleep with Ansley, but he didn't want them to do it just because the bond wouldn't be complete otherwise. And what about the spell? If that was the way Ansley wanted to do things, did it mean they had to cast the spell again? It might have been cast when Parker had been Byron, but how had the time spent apart and the loss of Parker's memories influenced that?

Now probably was the worst moment to ask the mages. If Carlyle had truly come back, they needed to find out and get ready to fight him.

Even though it probably wouldn't do them any good considering the circumstances. Parker needed to ask someone all of these questions, and while he should ask Ansley, he wasn't sure that was the best idea.

But what else could he do?

Ansley didn't want to investigate, but he couldn't look away from the burned spot on the map.

It was his duty to go. He needed to protect the other mages, since he was the only one who had his dragon back, even though it terrified him. The problem was that he didn't know what Parker would think about this. It would be within his right to refuse to go. He didn't remember any of his training, which meant it would be dangerous for both of them.

"We'll talk about it in the morning," Jarvis said, his tone uncompromising.

Tyne glared. "We have to act now. If Carlyle is free, we need to find him."

"And what do you expect Ansley to do if he goes there and Carlyle is free? Should he fight him on his own? Or with his dragon, who doesn't remember anything, not even his name?"

Tyne looked away. Ansley understood why he was panicking, and he felt the same. He was afraid of going there and finding out what had happened, and he didn't want to have to see Carlyle ever again, but someone had to do something.

Jarvis was right. Doing it tonight wouldn't help anyone, so it would be better for all of them to go back to bed. Ansley didn't know if he could. No one would care if he spent a few hours in his office, although he wasn't sure what he'd do. He just knew that even if he went to bed, he wouldn't be able to fall back asleep.

"Let's all go back to bed," Jarvis said, looking around. "I know you're scared. I am, too, and I don't want Carlyle to be back. Whatever happened tonight, it's not going to change while we sleep. At least if we wait until tomorrow, we can be slightly more ready. Besides, Ansley will have to tell Parker about this, and we don't know how he'll react or what he'll agree to. We can't be sure he'll want to go with Ansley."

"He's supposed to protect Ansley," Penley whispered. "Why wouldn't he go?"

"Because there's a difference between what he's supposed to do and what he can do," Ansley said. "He doesn't remember being a shield. He doesn't remember how to protect me."

"You can't go without him."

"I'm not going to unless he says he doesn't want to come."

Penley took a step forward. "If he doesn't want to go with you, I'll come. I might not be a dragon, but I can still protect you."

"There's no reason for us to talk about this tonight," Jarvis interjected. "Everyone, go back to bed. Get some rest, because we might have to face Carlyle in the morning. Hopefully, it was just someone taking down a few of the wards we placed on the stone, but it's no use talking about it now. We'll have a meeting in the morning, ask Parker what he thinks, and take it from there."

None of them wanted to face Carlyle again, and Ansley couldn't help but wonder what they'd do if he was free. The last time, they'd only managed to trap him because they'd had their dragons. They'd been able to use the dragons' magic, but they wouldn't have that advantage this time. They only had Parker, and while Ansley could probably use his magic even though Parker didn't know how it worked, the dragons were there for more than just that.

This entire thing was a mess, and Ansley didn't know how to get out of it.

Even though he loved his brothers, he was relieved when they started leaving the office. He wasn't surprised when Tyne wrapped an arm around Penley's shoulders and guided him out, gently whispering to him. Penley was the softest of them, and he'd had a hard time dealing with Carlyle the first time around. It would hurt him a lot to have to go through it a second time, but unfortunately, they didn't have a choice. If Carlyle was free, they had to take care of him, whether they liked it or not.

And this time, they couldn't afford to let him live.

Jarvis was the last one in the office. He stared at Ansley, and Ansley stared back. He knew how Jarvis felt. He felt the same way.

"I don't know what to do," Jarvis admitted.

"I don't think any of us expect you to."

"I'm the oldest. I've always been kind of a big brother to all of you, and I feel responsible."

"Maybe so, but we're all adults. We can contribute."

Jarvis nodded. "I hate having to ask you and Parker to go. You're not ready."

Ansley couldn't deny that. "We'll do what we can. It's no use worrying about it until we find out what happened."

"If you can convince Parker to do this, you can go with him tomorrow morning. If you need anything, call us, and we'll be there. We're not letting you face Carlyle alone, but it's better not to put ourselves in danger when we don't have our shields to protect us. It would be too much work for Parker alone."

"I never expected you to make me do this alone."

Jarvis gave Ansley a tight smile before heading for the door, too. He left it open in a silent order for Ansley to go to bed, but Ansley didn't think he could. His heart was still racing over what had happened tonight, even though he couldn't be sure Carlyle was free. He wouldn't be able to sleep, and he doubted he'd be able to work, either. What was left for him to do?

Getting to his feet, he decided to go to the library. Maybe losing himself in some books would help, and even if it didn't, it would pass some time. It was better than going back to bed and staring at the ceiling for hours.

He turned the lights off as he went. He expected the library to be dark when he reached it, but instead, he saw light coming from the slightly open door. He frowned and wondered which one of his brothers was there. He was ready to get whoever it was back to bed.

But it wasn't one of the mages. When Ansley walked in, it was to find Parker sitting by the empty fireplace. He looked up at Ansley and blinked, as if he'd been so focused on the book he was reading that he hadn't heard him.

"What are you doing here?" Ansley asked.

Parker rubbed his face with both his hands. "I couldn't sleep after what happened. Did I bother you?"

"No. What do you mean that you couldn't sleep after what happened?"

"I felt something—something *magic*. It woke me up, and when I left my room, I saw all of you freaking out and rushing to your office. I followed and heard your explanation about Carlyle and the map thing. Is he really back?"

Ansley flopped into one of the empty armchairs by Parker's. "I don't know. His presence is stronger, but it doesn't necessarily mean he's back. It could be that whoever is tinkering with the stone has managed to take down a few wards. We won't know until we go there."

Parker nodded seriously. "When are we going, then?"

"None of us expect you to sacrifice yourself for this. You don't have to come if you don't feel ready for it."

"I'm a dragon. If you're going, I'm coming with you. Besides, isn't a mage stronger when he has his dragon with him?"

"Yes, but considering the circumstances, it's not exactly a great plan."

"Still. It won't do you any good to go on your own, and if I'm there, I can shift and use my dragon form to defend you. I won't let you get hurt."

Strangely, Ansley believed Parker. Even though Parker had no idea what he was doing in his human form or even in his dragon one, he'd try. Ansley had no doubt about that. Parker's dragon form was big and strong enough to do real damage, even if he didn't know how to use it in a battle.

"I mean, I'm not sure how we work together," Parker continued. "But I'm ready to try if you are."

"We'll find a way to make it work," Ansley reassured him. "Even though you don't remember, you've been a protector since the moment you were born. That was when the magic chose you for me, and that hasn't changed, even though you lost your memories. Your instincts are there. They're rough and untrained, but it doesn't mean they're useless."

Ansley prayed he wasn't lying to Parker. He didn't know what would happen, but he could tell Parker would blame himself if Ansley got hurt, and he didn't want him to.

Parker wanted to believe Ansley's reassurances that every-thing would be okay, but he wasn't sure he could. No matter what and who he was, he had no memories of anything. Could it really be as simple as his body remembering what to do when he was faced with danger? Could he risk that not being so? Not if it meant Ansley could get hurt. They had no idea how they worked together, danger or no danger. Ansley had been avoiding Parker, which meant they hadn't spent time together. Considering they were doing this tomorrow, maybe it was time to change that.

Parker put his book on the small table next to the armchair and got to his feet. Ansley looked up at him, his eyes widen-ing when Parker offered him his hand. Parker wasn't sure why he'd done that, but he was relieved when Ansley took it, even though he had no idea what Parker was doing.

To be honest, neither did Parker.

He pulled Ansley to his feet. A plan was forming in his mind, and he hoped Ansley would go along with it.

"What are we doing?" Ansley asked when Parker pulled him toward the door.

"We're going to fly together."

Ansley pulled back on Parker's hand, but they didn't stop moving. Parker looked behind to check whether Ansley was freaking out or if he was okay with this and just wanted an explanation.

"What do you mean?" Ansley asked.

"We need to know if we can work together. We only have a few hours before going there tomorrow morning, which means we have to do it now."

"And you think that flying together is a good idea?"

"I don't see why not. I'll shift, and you can ride me. That way, we'll see if it's too awkward for me or if I can get used to it."

"You don't remember me riding you." Ansley's voice was soft.

"I don't remember anything."

Parker had never let anyone on his dragon, mostly because no one had known about it. Matthias had hinted at Parker shifting in front of him and showing him his dragon several times since he'd found out, but Parker had refused, afraid of his reaction. Mathias knew Parker was a dragon, but what would he do when he saw it with his own two eyes?

Besides, it felt right to have Ansley do this with him. Parker wanted him to be the first to ride him, even though he didn't understand why. His dragon was happy with that, and he was pretty sure it would have somehow pushed Matthias down if he'd tried climbing on the dragon's back. The dragon liked Matthias, but this was Ansley, their mage.

Ansley was silent as they left the library and walked down the hallways to the door. There were many doors in the castle, but Parker knew this one opened on one of the courtyards. He'd be able to shift there, and once he was in his dragon form, it would be easy for him to take to the air.

He'd always wondered how shifting worked. The fact that it was magic didn't answer any of his questions, but maybe he didn't need them answered. Shifting was what he did. He was a dragon shifter, and he didn't need a reason to be one or an explanation as to how it worked. He just did what he was supposed to do.

Once they were in the courtyard, he dropped Ansley's hand and placed himself in the middle. He didn't have to strip like the shifters in some of the books he'd read did, and he was grateful for that. He suspected it was because his shift depended on magic, and since he was supposed to protect Ansley, it would make sense for him to be dressed when he shifted back and forth rather than appear in his human form naked in the middle of a battlefield.

That would have been awkward.

It had been a while since he'd been in his dragon form. He hadn't shifted often back home because he hadn't wanted to risk anyone seeing him, but here, he didn't have to fear that. He'd still been hesitant to shift, mostly because of Matthias but also because all of this was new. Now, he realized how stupid he'd been. He could have shifted the first day, and no one would have said anything.

Well, except maybe Matthias, but he wasn't here now.

After his shift, Parker stretched out his neck and his wings. He elongated his spine, grinning like an idiot at the sensation. There was a slight breeze, and it moved over his skin as if the wind was welcoming him home.

"It's been a long time since I last saw you like this," Ansley murmured.

He reached for Parker's snout but stopped before touching him. He started moving his hand back as if he expected Parker not to want to be touched. Maybe Byron hadn't wanted it, but Parker? He wanted nothing more, so he pushed his snout against Ansley's palm. Ansley laughed, clearly surprised, and Parker huffed, sending warm air to Ansley's face.

Ansley grimaced. "No dragon breath, please."

Parker grinned at him, exposing his many teeth. Thankfully, Ansley didn't seem to be afraid of him. That made sense, since he'd known Parker as a dragon for a long time, even when Parker hadn't been with him. He wasn't afraid because he knew there was nothing to be afraid of.

Ansley took his time stroking Parker's cheeks and nose, then ran his fingertips down Parker's flank. Parker lowered himself flat on the ground, his belly pressed against the cool stones. He wanted to make this as easy as possible for Ansley, who would need a boost up on his back. Parker wasn't sure how to do it, but Ansley clearly did because he didn't hesitate.

He used Parker's knee and his wing to climb onto Parker's back. He moved as if he knew what he was doing, and Parker realized that while *he* couldn't remember them doing this, Ansley did. He moved like this because it wasn't the first time they'd flown together.

Ansley tightened his knees on Parker's back. Parker could feel him touch the spikes there, grabbing one of them with both his hands. He wondered if they'd used a saddle back then. That felt safer than flying like this, although even if Ansley was bucked off Parker's back, Parker would be fast enough to grab him before he splattered on the ground. Still, it was one more thing to ask Ansley about, and Parker made a mental note to remember to do so once he was back to his human form.

"Not too high," Ansley said. "We're not equipped for a crazy flight."

But eventually they would be, and Parker found himself strangely excited by that. He wanted to do this with Ansley. He wanted to do much more with Ansley, and sometimes, he wondered if it was because of the bond.

After what he'd read, he suspected that magic itself had intended for dragons and mages to be together. What could give the dragons a bigger incentive to keep the mages safe than to be in love with them? It made sense, which was why Parker had asked himself if the magic bond between dragons and mages also caused them to fall in love.

Or maybe they wanted to be together because of the reason the magic chose them for each other. There had to be one, even though Parker didn't know what it was. The only thing he did know for sure was that he wanted to spend time with Ansley and that he wanted to make him happy. He would never let anything happen to him, and he'd rather die than allow Ansley to be hurt. Whether that was because he was Ansley's shield or because the bond was pulling him toward falling in love, he didn't know.

And he didn't really care.

Who cared why he felt this way? There was no changing it, and that was fine with him. What would happen would happen.

And in the meantime, he and Ansley would fly.

CHAPTER TEN

L ast night had been incredible. After Ansley and Parker had flown, Ansley had stumbled back to his bedroom and fallen into bed. He'd fallen asleep in seconds, only to wake up this morning with Tyne banging on his door.

This morning was nowhere near as nice as last night had been. They had their meeting over breakfast, with Matthias blinking and staring at them owlishly. He hadn't noticed anything weird last night, and he'd had a few questions, but thankfully, he'd seemed to understand how serious the situation was, and he hadn't pushed for answers. He'd let the mages and their one dragon do what they needed to do, but Ansley had been able to tell he was worried about Parker. When he'd understood that Parker was supposed to go on this mission, he'd leaned closer and whispered something in Parker's ear.

Ansley had looked away then.

He still wasn't sure what to think of Matthias and Parker. Parker had insisted they were just friends, and Ansley wanted to believe him, but the part of him that reminded him that Byron hadn't wanted him was always there. Why would Parker want to be with him when he had someone like Matthias in his life? Ansley was more of a bother than anyone wanted to deal with, and Byron had made sure to tell him that.

Sometimes, Ansley had wondered why the magic had put them together and if maybe it had made a mistake. Now that he knew Parker, he knew the magic hadn't been mistaken. If Byron had been like Parker from the beginning, things between him and Ansley would have gone much more smoothly. As it was, Ansley had hated Byron as much as he'd loved him.

But all of that was in the past. Ansley needed to stop thinking about Byron because he was never coming back.

Instead, he focused on opening the portal. It wasn't his specialty, but since he'd been the one to cast the seeking spell and find where the wave of magic from last night had originated, it would make casting a portal easier.

Or at least, Ansley hoped so.

They were gathered in one of the courtyards with everyone behind him. He could feel their gazes on his back, and it took everything he had not to run away screaming. He hated disappointing people, and he felt that that was all he'd done so far. He'd found a dragon, but only his, and he'd been unable to make the spell work again. He could tell Carlyle was up to something, but not whether he was free or what he and Parker would be walking in on. He was no good and wondered how the other mages hadn't realized that over the years.

A strong hand grabbed his shoulder and squeezed. He looked back to see that Parker, who'd been standing behind him, had moved closer. He looked back at Ansley and nodded, and that small gesture was enough for Ansley to manage to push the negative thoughts away.

Maybe he was a disappointment, but he was the only one who could do this right now.

He sucked in a breath, thrust out both arms, and closed his eyes. The map was in his pocket, but he didn't have to look at it to know where he needed to open the portal. He'd been staring at the map since last night.

He spoke the incantation, and when the magic raised its head, he reached out to mold it. To his surprise, he felt a push at his back. It was a strange sensation but one he knew well. It wasn't a physical touch but another kind of magic that wanted to help.

Ansley opened up and allowed it to.

Parker might not remember anything, but his instincts knew what he should do. Or maybe it was his dragon, but either way, it was enough. Parker gave Ansley a much-needed boost, both of magic and confidence, and when Ansley blinked his eyes open, it was to find a portal in front of them.

This morning, Ansley had used the Internet to check the area where Carlyle was possibly located. The spell had isolated the house, so Ansley had focused the portal on the back yard. That way, no one would see them except maybe the people who lived there, and he suspected that they were the ones who had the stone and were trying to get Carlyle out of it, which meant they knew about magic.

He turned to look at Parker, who nodded at him. "The sooner we go, the sooner we'll be back," Parker said gently.

He was right, but Ansley wanted nothing less than to step through the portal. He didn't want to face Carlyle. None of them were ready, even though he had Parker. It would be a disaster if they had to fight Carlyle now, and Ansley felt he was leading Parker to his death.

But Parker gently pushed him toward the portal, and the only thing Ansley could do was go. He crossed it with Parker on his heels, and before closing it, he turned to look at his brothers one last time.

Matthias was there, too, and he looked as worried as the mages. Hopefully, the others would be able to keep him calm. It wouldn't help anyone for Matthias to freak out, especially not Parker.

But Ansley couldn't worry about Matthias. The only thing he should worry about was Carlyle and whether or not he was out of the stone, so he peered at the house.

It was an old Victorian house, and it had seen better days.

It was pretty but neglected, with overgrown plants in the garden and a porch that sank toward the right. The state of the place didn't tell Ansley much about the people who lived there.

"Now what?" Parker asked.

Ansley shrugged. "I guess we can knock?"

"Can you feel him?"

"No, but then I'm not casting the seeking spell right now."

"So you can't just feel other mages?"

"No." That meant there was no way for Ansley to know who was inside the house, which made him nervous. He prayed that when the door opened, he wouldn't find Carlyle standing there in front of him. He had no idea how he'd deal with it if it happened, and he hoped Parker had good reflexes.

They walked around the house, and Ansley almost expected someone to come out and ask what they were doing there. No one did, and they reached the front door without incident. He and Parker exchanged a glance, then Ansley raised a hand and knocked on the door.

"What are you going to tell whoever opens the door?" Parker asked.

"I don't know."

"Do we outright ask about the stone?"

Parker had a point. Ansley should have prepared a speech or something, but it was hard without knowing what he was about to face. Were the people who lived here mages actively trying to get Carlyle out of the stone, or was last night's event an accident? At this point, nothing would surprise him, but it would be hard to figure out just by looking at the person who opened the door.

The door swung open. Ansley sucked in a breath, words already on his lips. They were probably the wrong ones, but they died at the sight of the man standing before him.

It wasn't Carlyle.

Ansley's shoulders slumped in relief. This didn't mean Carlyle wasn't inside the house, but at least Ansley didn't have to face him yet.

"Yes?" the man asked, looking from Ansley to Parker.

"Hi." What else was Ansley supposed to say? "I'm Ansley."

The man cocked his head. "Graham. Do I know you?"

"I don't think so."

"Why are you here, then?"

What was Ansley supposed to say? Did he outright ask about the stone? Did Graham know about magic? Unfortunately, Ansley had no way to know if he was a mage or a human.

Thankfully, Parker took charge. He stepped forward, smiling at Graham. "Hi. I apologize for knocking on your door, but we were told that you might be the owner of an old family heirloom."

Graham frowned. "What heirloom?"

"It's a gemstone. It's not worth much, but it means a lot to Ansley's family." Parker looked at Ansley, and Ansley finally got himself under control.

He smiled at Graham. "Yes. It's red and quite chunky. It's not set in jewelry, or at least, it wasn't the last time I saw it."

Graham took a step back. "I don't know what you're talking about. I don't own anything like that."

He was lying. Ansley was sure of it, but it wasn't like he could accuse Graham to his face.

Right?

"What's going on?" a man asked from deeper inside the house.

Ansley heard footsteps, and the other man appeared. From his appearance, he was probably Graham's brother. His expression was harsh, though, and he didn't look anywhere as confused as Graham.

"Hi," Ansley said, hoping to charm him. "We're looking

for a family heirloom."

"We don't have anything that belongs to you."

"Simon, they want the stone," Graham whispered.

Unfortunately for him, he said it loud enough that Ansley heard him.

At the very least, they were in the right place. Graham had proved that by mentioning that they wanted the stone. He didn't know whether to be more relieved or more frightened.

Who were these guys? Why did they have the stone in which Carlyle was supposed to be stuck? Even more importantly, had they managed to get Carlyle out of the stone, or were they just trying for now?

Parker needed answers to those questions, and he needed them ASAP.

"You're an idiot," Simon snapped to his brother.

Parker didn't know for sure that they were brothers, but if he had to bet on it, he would. They looked like each other enough that there was no way they weren't related.

"Sorry," Graham murmured, his gaze dropping to the floor.

Parker kept a smile on his face. "Look, I understand you don't know us, but we just want the gemstone. It's an important heirloom for Ansley's family." And Parker trusted Ansley's spell. If the spell said the stone was here, that meant it was, no matter what Graham and Simon were trying to convince them of.

Simon crossed his arms over his chest. "We don't have any gemstones."

"It would be great if you could check."

"I don't need to."

Parker was losing his patience, but what could he do? "Look, we know it's here." He didn't mention magic, even though he suspected it wouldn't have come as a surprise to Simon. "Just give it to us. We'll leave, and you'll never see us again."

Simon pushed his brother away from the door and stepped out. "I'm not giving you anything." His eyes narrowed, and he looked at Ansley. "You're one of them, aren't you?"

"One of who?" Ansley asked.

Parker's instincts fired up. He lunged for Ansley, but he wasn't sure he'd make it in time. Simon had reached for something just inside the door. He raised his hand and threw himself at Ansley.

He had a knife.

Parker roared, the sound not nearly as impressive in his human form as it was in his dragon form, but he didn't care. It was enough to send Graham running, which was what he'd wanted.

Well, one of the things he'd wanted.

Simon was still with, them, and just like Parker had feared, he'd been too late. The knife had sunk into Ansley's arm, and Simon was already sliding it out, no doubt to stab him again.

Parker wouldn't allow him to do that.

He grabbed Simon by the back of his shirt and pulled him away from Ansley. His dragon was pushing to come out, but Parker didn't allow it to. They were too exposed and couldn't afford for the neighbors to notice what was happening. Parker could imagine the panic if someone were to look out their window and see a massive dragon eating Simon.

Simon turned his attention to Parker, apparently not caring about his neighbors. He raised the knife and screamed as he launched himself at Parker.

It was the first time Parker faced a man with a knife, or at least the first time he remembered having to do so. His body moved almost on its own, and he easily sidestepped Simon. He grabbed Simon's wrist and raised his knee simultaneously, slamming them together, causing Simon to scream in pain. Simon's hand spasmed, and he dropped the knife.

Parker slammed him against the wall. He pressed his arm against Simon's throat, pushing hard enough to make it impossible for him to breathe. He leaned close, ready to kill Simon if he as much as looked at Ansley the wrong way.

"Parker," Ansley said.

It knocked Parker out of whatever state he was in. He stepped away from Simon, who slid down the wall, clutching at his throat. Parker didn't recognize himself, but he'd have time to break down over that later. When he turned to look at Ansley, he saw the blood on Ansley's arm, and he freaked out all over again.

He rushed over to the mage leaning against the wall on the other side of the door from Simon. "Ansley?"

Ansley shook his head. "I'll be fine."

"You're bleeding."

"Yeah, but it's just my arm. I'm not going to die."

The thought that Ansley could die made Parker's chest ache. He cupped Ansley's face with both his hands and pulled him closer, not thinking about how Ansley might react to a kiss.

Thankfully, Ansley didn't push Parker away. His eyes widened, but when their lips met, he pushed closer instead of leaning away. He leaned into the kiss, and Parker's heart exploded.

Ansley wanted him.

Even though Parker wanted nothing more than to strip Ansley naked and make him his right here and now, he couldn't. They were still in danger, so Parker stepped away as soon as his dragon had been reassured that Ansley was all right. He turned to Simon, not one bit surprised to see the man had vanished.

Dammit.

Ansley hadn't expected to be kissed. To be fair, he also hadn't expected to be wounded, and he could have done without that. His arm hurt like a bitch, but would he have gotten kissed by Parker if he hadn't been wounded?

Parker took a step back. His eyes were wide as he looked at Ansley, and Ansley stared because how could he not? Unfortunately, it didn't last nearly long enough, because Parker turned to the open door and peeked inside.

No sounds were coming from the house. That freaked Ansley out, especially when Parker took a step inside.

"What are you doing?" he asked.

"I'm going to see if I can find either of the two brothers."

"You don't even know if there's a ward on the house."

Parker hesitated. "Is there?"

"I don't think so. I can't feel anything, and it would have activated when you walked in. Still, you can't go in there on your own."

"I'm not going to drag you inside. You're hurt."

"And you could be in danger. What made you think I'd let you go inside without me?"

They stared at each other. If Ansley had been dealing with Byron, he'd have expected him to go even though Ansley had told him not to. Byron had known he wasn't invincible, but he'd also known he was strong and that he could defend himself. Ansley was sure Parker could, too, but not in the same way, and he was terrified of what could happen if Parker went in. He didn't want to lose him, especially not after that kiss.

He still needed to ask what it meant, dammit.

Parker's shoulders slumped. "Fine. You're right."

Ansley blinked. "I am?"

"There are only the two of us, and it would be too easy for

you to get hurt again. I can't risk going inside and Simon and Graham coming out and killing you."

Ansley should probably be pissed that Parker didn't believe he could defend himself, but he wasn't. They'd hammered in that he was Ansley's protection, and Ansley didn't think he'd seen him do much magic. He'd been focused on fixing the seeking spell, and of course, on avoiding Parker. Maybe that hadn't been the best idea, and Ansley would have to rectify that. He hadn't been helpless for a hundred years or before meeting Byron.

As soon as his arm stopped feeling like it was about to fall off.

He moved and winced, and Parker was instantly by his side. "What can I do?"

"I don't want to leave without poking around and at least trying to find the stone, but it kind of hurts. Maybe call the others? They'll be ready to come."

Parker nodded and took his phone out. He had all the mages on speed dial, and it only took a handful of seconds to call Jarvis and tell him what had happened. A few minutes later, the sound of running footsteps told Ansley they weren't alone anymore.

He just hoped it wasn't Simon and Graham coming to finish him or stab him in the other arm.

Luckily Penley appeared, running around the house, Tyne right behind him. Tyne looked pissed, and as soon as Penley slowed down, he grabbed his arm and pulled him back. Penley glared at him, shook his hand off, and started moving toward Ansley again.

"What are you doing?" Tyne asked.

"Getting to Ansley. He's hurt."

"You're going to get yourself killed if you don't make sure Ansley is alone first."

"He's not alone. He has Parker."

"You know what I mean."

"No one's come out of the house since I called you," Parker said.

That was enough for Penley, who rushed toward the porch steps and climbed them two by two. He dropped to his knees next to Ansley, who had to sit down, both because of how relieved he was and because of the pain.

This was supposed to be simple, dammit. He and Parker just needed to poke around a bit and find out if Carlyle was free.

"What happened? What did they do to you? Was it Carlyle?" Penley's mouth was working, but so were his hands.

He'd brought a backpack with him, and it was open. He kept taking things out but hadn't reached for Ansley's arm yet. He'd always been a little impulsive, which explained why he was already here while the others were only now appearing around the corner of the house.

Jarvis looked pissed enough to kill Simon if he ever got his hands on him. "What happened?" he asked, his hands already in the air as he cast a ward around Ansley and Penley.

Ansley licked his lips. "I'm not sure. The seeking spell said the stone was in this house, so we knocked. A guy opened— Graham. He was flustered and kept telling us that he had no idea what we were talking about when we asked about the stone. Then another guy appeared, probably his brother. Graham said something that confirmed he knew about the stone, and his brother called him an idiot. He attacked."

Jarvis nodded. "Which is how you ended up wounded."

"Yes. Parker slammed him against the wall, then focused on making sure I was all right. That's when Simon went back inside, and neither of them has come out again."

Jarvis peered inside the house. "All right. Penley, stay here and take care of Ansley. Tyne and I will go in."

"You're not going without us," Keylon said, glaring at

Jarvis.

"I'm coming with you, too," Parker said.

"Your place is with Ansley," Jarvis told him.

"I agree, but he's inside a ward for now. If either of the brothers appears, he and Penley can scream, and we'll hear them."

"We don't know what's inside the house. There could be a ward so that no one can hear what happens inside, or that makes it so that we can't leave once we're in."

"You're going in?"

"I have to."

"Then I'm coming with you. I might not be your shield, but I can still protect you."

Parker and Jarvis stared at each other for a moment. Ansley wished Parker would look at him instead, but he was trying to get Jarvis to change his mind. Ansley wasn't sure how he felt about that. He was selfish and wanted Parker to stay with him, but he also didn't want Jarvis to get hurt. There was no way to know what—or who—they'd find inside. Sending Jarvis and Tyne on their own might mean they never came back, and that wasn't something Ansley was ready for.

Jarvis eventually nodded. "You'll stick with us. We'll cast wards, so hopefully, if there's anything that shouldn't be there, we'll be protected. We're looking for the stone."

"What about the brothers?" Tyne asked. He looked ready to charge into the house, which, knowing him, wasn't a surprise.

"Are they mages?" Jarvis asked Ansley.

Penley had been poking at the wound in Ansley's arm since he'd arrived, and listening to the conversation helped distract Ansley. Now that the attention was on him, he felt the pain all too keenly. "I don't know. Neither of them tried casting any spell."

"It doesn't mean they're not mages."

"No, but what do you do when you're threatened? You get ready to cast a spell because it's how you've learned to defend yourself. Besides, I can't feel any kind of ward on this place."

Jarvis nodded and pressed a hand on the side of the house. He whispered a few words, and everyone waited for whatever he was about to say.

They'd never elected him as their leader or anything official, but they didn't need to. Maybe it was because he was older, but they'd all looked up to him almost since the beginning. He'd been the one to gather them after he'd realized how much of a problem Carlyle had become. He'd always felt guilty because Carlyle had been his apprentice, but Ansley didn't see it like that. Jarvis couldn't have changed Carlyle or what he'd done. He'd taught Carlyle how to use magic, but if it hadn't been him, it would have been someone else. Carlyle was bent on getting what he wanted, and that was becoming a powerful mage. They still weren't quite sure how he'd managed, but Ansley had a few ideas, and all of them made him want to throw up.

Jarvis eventually nodded. "Tyne, Parker, Keylon, you're coming with me. Penley and Dallin, stay here. Take care of Ansley, and if anyone comes out, scream for us."

"I'll make sure neither of them gets hurt," Dallin said with a vigorous nod.

Ansley glanced at Parker, but Parker avoided looking at him. Did he regret the kiss? Maybe that was why he was running into danger. He didn't want Ansley to talk about it, and leaving felt easier. There was little Ansley could do. He had questions. He wanted to ask Parker why he'd kissed him and what it meant, but now wasn't the right moment to do that.

Parker stepped closer, and Ansley wasn't sure what to expect.

"I'm sorry."

Ansley stared as Parker stepped back and followed Jarvis

inside the house. Well, he hadn't known what to expect, but it certainly hadn't been for the man who'd kissed him to apologize for it.

Parker didn't know what else to do. All his instincts were fired up, telling him to protect Ansley. Ansley was Parker's mage, and he'd been wounded, which meant Parker and his dragon weren't doing their job.

If the only reason he was here was to protect Ansley, and Ansley had been hurt, Parker hadn't done what he was supposed to do. He needed to atone, to show Ansley and the others that he could be what they needed.

He also wanted to get his hands on Simon and give him a good shake.

Even though he wanted nothing more than to charge inside the house, he followed Jarvis's lead. The mage knew what he was doing, and they really should have talked about this before Parker and Ansley came on this mission. Parker had a lot of questions about being a dragon and a shield—how it worked, and what he was supposed to do—but he'd never thought about asking the mages what their roles were in these fights. There was no way they were as vulnerable as Parker felt, and he needed to remember that they could use magic in a way he could barely imagine.

Jarvis and Tyne were the first inside the house. Keylon was right behind Parker, and they moved like a team. No one suggested they go off on their own, for which Parker was glad. Even though he was Ansley's shield, he felt the need and duty to protect the other mages, too.

"Tell me what you think of the situation," Jarvis quietly ordered as he stepped into a living room.

It was empty, but Parker stayed tense. "I think Simon and Graham are brothers. The one in charge is Simon, and he's also the one who hurt Ansley, which means he's dangerous."

"I'm going to kick his ass," Tyne said with a growl.

He'd have to get in line, because Parker would be the first to kick Simon's ass.

"You can do all the ass-kicking you want later. We need to find out if the stone is here first," Jarvis said as he raised a hand.

Parker felt a small wave of something tickle his skin, so he knew Jarvis was using magic. It was odd, because it wasn't visible, but it was effective, and when Jarvis shook his head, they knew they wouldn't find anything in this room.

They walked through the house without finding anyone, which was explained when they reached the kitchen and found the back door wide open. The two brothers had clearly run away through there, and Parker turned to Jarvis. "Did you guys see anyone when you arrived?"

"No, which is strange. We would have noticed two guys running out of the house."

Parker looked around. "Is it possible they're still around?"

"I'm going to cast a seeking spell," Keylon declared.

Parker inched closer to him in case he needed to be protected while he used magic. He could feel it again as Keylon muttered a spell. Parker was still a bit hesitant when it came to magic and how it worked, but clearly, it was time for him to get his head out of his ass and fully commit to what was happening. Either he was in and he'd train to be Ansley's shield, or he got the fuck out and left the mages to deal with this on their own.

He already knew which one he'd choose.

He wasn't going anywhere, and it wasn't just because of Ansley. A lot of it was him, but Parker liked the other mages, and he enjoyed feeling like he was part of a family in a way he couldn't remember ever being. But Ansley was precious. He needed to be protected at all costs, and Parker and his dragon were up for the task. It was theirs because magic had chosen it to be, and Parker wanted to make Ansley proud.

He also wanted to kiss him again.

He shouldn't have done it. He'd been terrified after seeing Simon's attack and Ansley bleeding, and he'd acted instinctively. He and his dragon had needed to reassure themselves that Ansley was okay, and that had felt like the best way to do so. Parker hated that he'd forced a kiss on Ansley, though. He doubted Ansley had been thinking about kisses at that moment, and even worse, Ansley was in pain. He hadn't deserved to be mauled by Parker, which was why Parker had apologized before leaving him on the porch with the other two.

"I don't like this," Tyne muttered as he walked ahead, the magic he used almost a solid presence in front of him.

Probably none of them liked anything about the situation.

"This wasn't your fault," Jarvis told Parker as they continued exploring the house.

"I was here to protect Ansley. He got hurt. Whose fault is it?" Parker told him as he looked into the bedroom.

"The fault of the guy who hurt him. You might be a shield, but that doesn't mean you're invincible."

"No, but it does mean I should be good at what I do. Why am I even here if I don't know how to protect Ansley?"

"I realize you've been feeling lost and trying to find a reason for all of this, but you're here because you and Ansley are linked. It doesn't matter that you're the first shield back. It doesn't matter that you don't know what you're doing. That'll change in time, but not if you decide to leave."

Parker glared at Jarvis. "Who said I was leaving?"

Jarvis looked relieved. "I'm glad you're not. I understand why you're scared, and I am, too. But we'll find a way out of this. We did the last time we had to face Carlyle, and we will this time, too."

Parker could only nod. He wanted to kick Carlyle's ass and, even more, Simon's. "Do you know anything about the brothers?"

"No. When we dealt with Carlyle the last time, he worked alone."

Something about that tickled at Parker's brain, but he couldn't quite get to what the problem was. It was something worth thinking about, though. "They didn't look much older than their twenties, if even that. Is it possible they don't have anything to do with him?"

"Considering they know about the stone, I doubt it."

"Maybe they own the stone but don't know what it is. How did they get their hands on it, anyway?"

"I don't know, but I'll find out."

Jarvis's tone was convincing, and Parker believed him. Jarvis wanted this to be over as much as Parker and the mages. They were ready for Carlyle to be out of their lives forever, and while it would take time, it helped to have something to work toward.

What would help even more was to have more dragons.

"We're not going to find anything here," Tyne said after they'd explored the last empty room upstairs.

"We haven't checked the basement," Parker pointed out.

The three of them looked at each other. It felt like a trap, but it didn't mean they wouldn't poke around there, too.

"You need to spend time with Ansley," Tyne curtly said as the three of them traipsed down the stairs, heading for the basement.

"Don't you think I've been trying to do just that?"

Tyne huffed. "He's got a crush on you, and yes, Jarvis, I know it's not my place to tell Parker, but someone needs to do something so they both get their heads out of their asses."

Jarvis glared, but he didn't try to stop Tyne from speaking.

Parker was glad. It had always been hard to talk to Ansley,

and he felt Tyne was giving him a peek into why Ansley was the way he was.

"It's not the first time I've seen him behave this way," Tyne continued. "But he's going to push you away unless you push back. He and Byron had a complicated thing going on. Byron was a dickhead, but I don't think you are."

Parker wasn't sure what to say. "Thank you."

Tyne snorted. "I said I don't *think* you're a dickhead. Don't prove me wrong, yeah? Don't hurt Ansley."

Parker had no intention of doing that, but he wasn't sure there would be a choice. Sometimes, people hurt each other even if they didn't mean to do so.

Ansley was fragile, and finding out more about Byron had told Parker why. He hated that his old self had hurt Ansley, but he wasn't sure if there was anything he could do to fix it or even if he should try.

But the very least he could do was talk to Ansley. After the kiss, they needed to clear things up and decide where they'd go from there and what they both wanted to happen. There was no way to know if Ansley would want Parker to kiss him again, but now that Parker allowed himself to think about it, it felt like Ansley had been happy to be kissed.

Or maybe he'd been in too much pain to push Parker away. Parker was going to have to find out, and he wasn't sure he was ready for that.

CHAPTER ELEVEN

They were right back where they'd started.

Ansley had insisted on staying at the house until he was sure Parker and the others were okay. That meant that until they came out, he'd sat on the porch with Penley and Dallin hovering next to him and trying to convince him to leave.

How could Ansley have gone home when he didn't know what was going on? It had been his job to find out whether or not Carlyle had been freed of the stone, but he hadn't been able to do even that. Jarvis hadn't given him many details, but he'd explained they'd found the house empty, including the basement, the mention of which, for some reason, had made Tyne shudder. Jarvis had guided all of them away and back home, promising he'd tell them everything he'd found once they were safe.

Ansley had been relieved to leave that place. He didn't know if Carlyle had anything to do with it, but he didn't feel comfortable there after being stabbed. To be fair, he hadn't felt comfortable there even before being stabbed, but he couldn't help but wonder if Simon was hiding somewhere, staring at him and planning how to stab him again.

If he thought about it logically, Ansley knew it the possibility was remote. Simon had panicked. He'd been trying to protect himself and his secret, but now that he was gone, he had no reason to stab Ansley again. There wasn't a reason for Ansley to stab him, either, but he wanted to do just that every time he moved, and he'd felt like that through his shower and as he dressed.

"You should have stayed in your room," Parker said as he hovered next to Ansley.

Ansley glared at him. "This meeting is for everyone involved, isn't it?"

"Yes, but you were stabbed. You need to rest."

"What I need is to find out what was in the house." And what Parker had been thinking, kissing him, but there would be time for that later.

Hopefully.

Ansley had been the one to avoid Parker before, but he wondered if Parker would now avoid him. He seemed especially on edge. Had Parker kissed him because he thought he was dying or something? It certainly felt like he was, but he'd been stabbed in the arm, not the heart. No matter how much pain he was in, he'd be perfectly fine in a week or two.

Jarvis cleared his throat, getting everyone's attention. They were gathered in the room they used as a conference room. It was also where they worked together when they needed to, and the space was dominated by a massive wooden table surrounded by chairs. Only the mages and Parker were here, although they were ready to bring in the assistants if they had to. Ansley would rather keep Etta out of it, though. She was human, which meant she couldn't defend herself the way Ansley could. Without knowing whether or not Carlyle was back, Ansley wasn't willing to put her at risk. It wouldn't be that much of a risk as long as they stayed in the castle, but still. He hadn't been able to defend himself. What was to say he'd be able to defend Etta?

"We didn't find much in the house," Jarvis explained. "There were signs of someone attempting to do magic in the basement, but I believe whoever tried is human."

"How does that even work?" Parker asked.

"Humans can use magic. It's much harder for them than it is for mages, of course, but as long as they have the right tools, they can do it."

"Did they have the right tools?"

Jarvis hesitated, then grimaced. "From what I saw, yes. I'm not sure how they knew what they were doing, but they did." Jarvis looked around the table. "I didn't see the stone anywhere, but I did find fragments of it on a table."

Ansley sucked in a breath. "Maybe they tried to open it manually," he said.

"And when they couldn't, they tried using magic," Jarvis confirmed. "I don't know if what we felt the other night was Carlyle being released or just a few of the wards falling, but we won't be able to find out if we don't get the stone."

"Wouldn't Carlyle have contacted us if he were free?" Keylon asked. "I mean, I didn't know him well, but he never struck me as a modest person. If he was free, he'd want us to know."

Jarvis nodded. "I suspect you're right. Either he's still in the stone, or he's trying to get used to the world as it is now."

Because while the mages had been free to move around for the past hundred years, Carlyle had been stuck in the stone. He had no idea what cell phones were or what most technology was. It would be hard for him to wrap his mind around everything without freaking out, although having two humans with him would probably help.

"Maybe he's still stuck, then," Penley said, sounding hopeful.

He kept glancing at Ansley as if he was afraid Ansley was about to faint or something. Ansley would have rolled his eyes if he hadn't known it came from a good place. Penley was worried about Ansley, even though he'd stitched the wound in his arm and had used magic to ensure no infection occurred. He'd also boosted the healing a bit, but it would be better for Ansley's body to do that by itself.

Unfortunately for Ansley.

"We have to think as if he's already out," Tyne interjected. "Either he's out right now, or he will be soon. He has two minions, which means there's someone who can get him out of the stone."

"Even if they're human?" Parker asked.

"There were several things we never recovered that belonged to Carlyle," Jarvis explained. "Including his grimoires. We have no way to know what kind of spell he created or what he wrote down, which means that whoever got those books might have the instructions to get him out of the stone."

"But he wasn't the one who trapped himself in there. How would these people know how to deal with the spell you cast?"

"It would take them a while to study the magic and come up with a solution, but they've had a hundred years."

There was no way Graham and Simon were even fifty. Ansley would be surprised if they were over thirty, but that didn't mean they hadn't been working on this for a while. It also didn't mean they hadn't taken over for someone who'd been working on it for years. Carlyle had worked alone, but he had minions.

They'd always wondered if one of them had found the stone when they'd all been passed out. They'd hoped it hadn't been one of them, and they'd relaxed after nothing had happened for a while and Carlyle had remained trapped.

Clearly, they shouldn't have.

"We should assume he's free," Tyne insisted. "That way, we won't be surprised when he finally pops out. I don't care who he's working with. He's the dangerous one, and he's the one we have to fight."

"How do we fight him without our dragons?" Dallin asked.

"Carefully," Jarvis told him. "We'll have to reinforce the wards around the castle. The more magical protection we have, the safer we'll be. I don't want us to be stuck in the castle while Carlyle attacks us, but even if he's free, I doubt he'll come here right away. For one, the castle is shielded from seeking spells, so he can't find us. He'll also be too weak to do anything that can hurt us."

"What about his dragon?" Parker suddenly asked.

Everyone turned to him. "What?" Ansley asked.

"When you found me, you told me that every mage has a dragon. The magic chooses them for each other, right? Who did the magic choose for Carlyle? Even though he's the big bad guy now, he was Jarvis's apprentice first. Didn't he have a shield back then?"

Ansley hadn't realized they hadn't told him about Carlyle's shield. "He did, but no one knows what happened to him. One day, he vanished, and that's more or less when Carlyle started going nuts. In the beginning, we thought that maybe something had happened to him that had made Carlyle the way he was, but honestly, I'm not sure anymore. I wouldn't be surprised if Carlyle did something to him."

"That's possible?"

Ansley shrugged. "Everything is possible with Carlyle. He won't have help from his dragon, though." That was a good thing for them, but it had been years since Ansley had thought of the dragon, and again he wondered what had happened to him. He felt they should have helped him, even though no one had known how deeply disturbed Carlyle was.

Once again, they had no idea what was happening, which made it almost impossible to plan and protect themselves and each other.

Parker wasn't surprised that something had happened to Carlyle's dragon, but he was curious. How could a dragon disappear like that? Magic had to have been involved, and he didn't think any of the mages he lived with had anything to do with it. Either the dragon had left Carlyle because Carlyle had gone mad, or something had happened to him. If that was true, had Carlyle been the one who did it?

Once again, Parker wished he knew more about his past. He'd been avoiding thinking about it too much and going through the things Ansley and the others had kept for him, but maybe it was time to take the plunge and do it.

Everything was in the attic. When the dragons had vanished, the mages had gathered their things and put them away for safekeeping until they returned. No one had imagined it would take more than a hundred years for that to happen, but Parker was here now. He didn't feel like that stuff was his anymore, probably because it hadn't been in a long time, and he wasn't anything like Byron. Hopefully, the stuff could give him a hint as to what to do about Carlyle, maybe even find a way to defeat the guy.

He could always hope.

When he'd fought Simon, he hadn't remembered what he was supposed to do, but he'd done it anyway. It was almost as if his body had a memory of its own, maybe at the muscular level. Or maybe it truly was his shield instincts. There was no way for him to know, but he needed to be able to replicate what had happened in case Ansley was attacked again. He needed those instincts to come back and to be able to do this even when they weren't in danger. That was the only way to keep himself trained enough that he'd be ready when they had to face the brothers again.

He stopped in the middle of the hallway on his way to the attic. Was there a spell to unlock memories? Penley had been looking into it, and every time Parker asked, he said he hadn't found anything new. That probably hadn't changed, but it couldn't hurt to ask again, right?

That was how much Parker didn't want to have to face

Byron. He turned around and headed for the hallway where the offices were located, not one bit eager to go to the attic.

His feet took him toward Ansley's office. Penley's was just a few doors away, but Parker couldn't make himself move. He stared at the closed door, wondering what Ansley was doing behind it.

Resting, hopefully, but Parker doubted it. Ansley infuriated him as much as he made him want to drag him into his bed. They still hadn't talked about the kiss, but it was something they needed to do, and soon. They wouldn't be able to focus on the fight with Carlyle if they were obsessing over the kiss.

Parker sighed and bumped his forehead against the door. He had no idea what he was doing, and he needed help. He could ask about all the memory spells in the world, but they wouldn't change the fact that Parker didn't have memories to unlock. Penley had told him that it was as if someone had torn those memories away, which would make sense. Carlyle would have wanted to hurt the dragons and the mages as much as he could, and what better way to make it so the dragons couldn't remember their mages?

He pushed away from the door, moved back down the hallway, and headed to the attic again. There would be no memory spell for him, which meant he needed to work on an alternative way to find out more about his past and how he could gain his training back. He didn't need to remember being Byron. He didn't *want* to remember being Byron. The guy had been a dickhead, and he hadn't deserved Ansley. Parker wasn't sure *he* deserved him, but he was going to work at it until he did. Keeping Ansley protected and safe was his job, but he couldn't forget the words he'd read in that book in the library.

Dragons and mages were supposed to be together. There had to be a reason for that, and even if it didn't give him back his memories, he wanted to find out what it was. He felt he knew something about it, but he couldn't remember it, just like he couldn't remember anything about his past. It had to be there somewhere, though, and he'd find it.

For Ansley's sake.

CHAPTER TWELVE

"I need your help."

Ansley looked up at his office door. Penley hovered there, looking unsure whether he should come in. Ansley was once again tinkering with the seeking spell, but it was just about time for a break.

"What's up?"

Penley rushed in, already explaining. "I know you're busy and that you're still in pain, but I've been poking around memory spells, and so far, nothing will work. I need to get Parker's memories back, and I was wondering if maybe you could help me tweak a spell. I've already chosen several, so we'll have to see which one is more easily changed, and I still can't make promises, but I thought it was worth a try."

Ansley tried to make sense of the many words. "You want to tweak a memory spell?"

"It's the only thing I haven't tried yet."

Ansley didn't want Penley to be disappointed. "I thought you said the memories just aren't there anymore."

"I could be wrong." Penley sounded like he hoped he was. "I thought about pulling Jarvis in, but I don't want to bother him. I know these past few days have been hard on him." Penley's eyes widened. "They've been hard on you, too, of course. How's your arm?"

Ansley waved Penley's worries away. "I'm fine."

"You're sure? Because if you're in pain, I can get you more painkillers."

"I don't need painkillers." Although maybe Ansley should

take more of them because his head was starting to pound. That was because the seeking spell still wasn't working, though. He needed to have a conversation with the magic, but it wasn't like the magic answered or anything like that.

Penley slumped into one of the chairs on the other side of Ansley's desk. "How are things going between you and Parker?"

The change in topic made the headache pound behind Ansley's eyes. "We're fine."

"Yeah? Why does he look like a kicked puppy, then?"

"I don't know what you're talking about." Ansley had been waiting for Parker to come to him and talk. He could be the one to take the first step and mention the kiss, but he had no idea where to start. He'd figured he'd let Parker do that, since he'd initiated the kiss, after all.

Penley stared at Ansley for a moment before rolling his eyes. "Really?"

"I truly don't. I'm not avoiding him anymore."

"Are you sure? Because you've been spending an awful lot of time in your office."

"I'm still working on the seeking spell, and besides, I'm still in some pain. I've been eating my meals with you, haven't I?"

"True. Don't think I haven't noticed you don't really talk to Parker when you're there, though."

"There's not much to talk about. Besides, you can see he's more comfortable with Matthias."

"They're not together."

"I'm aware. Matthias is Parker's best friend."

"He is, and he told me he talked to you."

Ansley's cheeks heated, and he looked out the window. He hadn't expected Matthias to keep the conversation a secret, but he also hadn't expected him to talk about it with Penley. "I'm not sure what you want from me."

"Give Parker a chance. He's not Byron."

"Don't you think I'm aware of that? Believe me, I, of all people, know he's not Byron and that he's nothing like him. That doesn't mean this is a good idea."

"Why not? Jarvis and Marlow made it work."

Ansley knew better than to ask about Penley's dragon. They'd been working things out, and everyone had been able to see they cared about each other. He'd been ripped away from Penley, and even though Penley tried to act as if he hadn't been hurt, all of them had been. Finding Parker was the first step to healing that pain, but there would never be a second step if Ansley didn't get his shit together.

He sighed. "I've been a bit distracted," he admitted.

"At least you're honest. It's just that the two of you give us hope, you know? You're the first of us to have your dragon back, and it's weird to watch you keep your distance from him. Then I remember how you were with Byron, and I understand better, but spending time with Parker showed me that Byron was just a memory. I doubt Parker will ever hurt you the way Byron did, especially intentionally."

"I don't expect him to. I'm just trying to work on everything at the same time, and it isn't easy."

Because Ansley wasn't just looking for the other dragons. He was also looking for the stone, Carlyle, and he'd been trying to find Simon and his brother, too. So far, none of the seeking spells he'd used had given him results, and he wasn't quite sure what to think about that. He was starting to think it was entirely his fault. Maybe he wasn't putting enough focus into the spells. It would be a logical explanation considering his thoughts kept drifting to Parker.

"Anyway, I was thinking about modifying a memory spell," Penley jumped to the next topic, or rather, jumped back to the reason he was here.

"We can certainly look into it. Give me all your research, and we'll get together tomorrow or the day after that."

Penley was excited again. "I can't wait."

"Modifying a spell might not work, and even if it does, it might not give Parker his memories back," Ansley warned.

"I know. I just need something to work on so I can distract myself. If I don't, I'll keep obsessing over Carlyle, and I don't want to think about him."

Ansley doubted anyone wanted to think about Carlyle, so he could understand. If he could help distract Penley, he was up for it. He could do with a distraction that wasn't Parker, at least for a few hours. Maybe working on something new would give him some distance, allowing him to see what was going wrong with the seeking spell.

When Penley left, Ansley took a few moments to gather his thoughts. He pulled his papers together, went over the seeking spell again, and decided to make a few more tweaks. He suspected that what he needed was the other mages' presence with him when he cast the spell. He'd been thinking about the various dragons like he had about Parker, but maybe he shouldn't be the one to cast the spell. He wanted to be because he knew it by heart, but having Jarvis by his side while he was trying to find Marlow could only help. So far, Ansley had refused to ask any of his friends to be present when he cast the spell because he didn't want them to be disappointed, but that was truly the only thing left, as far as he could see.

He got up from his chair and moved toward his worktable. If he was going to do this with Jarvis there, it had to be perfect. He put a mix of herbs together, getting it ready to burn. He had several lit candles on the surface, and one of them wobbled when he knocked his hip against the table. He managed to keep it upright, but just then, there was a quick knock on the door before it opened.

He turned around, unsure who was invading his space, and lost contact with the candle at the same time. It tilted toward the bowl with the herbs, and he knew what was going to happen before it did.

The candle tipped on its side, the flames licking the herbs. There was a whoosh of air, then a small explosion. Someone cried out, and two strong hands grabbed Ansley by the waist and pulled him away. He blinked, his ears feeling stuffed, his vision partially blinded by white lights.

"What happened?" Parker asked, appearing in front of Ansley. "Are you okay? I'm sorry if I distracted you. I didn't mean to, but you skipped lunch, and I wanted to make sure you were eating."

Ansley blinked again and tried to make sense of Parker's words. Why was everyone talking so much today? "I'm fine," he reassured Parker.

Parker stared down at him. "You're sure?"

"Pretty much. Why are you here?" Was he ready to talk about the kiss, or was he really just trying to feed Ansley?

Parker gestured at the desk, and when Ansley turned, it was to find a tray heavy with food waiting for him. His eyes prickled, and he told himself it was because of the explosion. It had to be it. There was no way Parker bringing him lunch was pushing him to tears.

Yet one tear rolled down his cheek, then another, and he had to bite on his lower lip hard so he wouldn't sob.

What the fuck was happening to him?

Parker wasn't sure what to do. He wanted to comfort Ansley, but he didn't know if the gesture would be welcome. Still, he wanted Ansley to step away from his work for a moment, relax and breathe, and hopefully, stop crying.

Hesitantly, he raised an arm and wrapped it around Ansley's shoulders. He didn't expect Ansley to break down against him or anything like that, but like this, Ansley was close enough that Parker could feel his breath against his skin.

It made him shiver, but thankfully, Ansley either didn't notice or didn't care.

Things wouldn't have been like this with Byron. Parker didn't know how to deal with a crying Ansley any more than Byron would have, but while Byron would have run out of the room as quickly as he could, Parker wasn't willing to do that. He wasn't Byron, and he hadn't been in a long time. He was Parker, and he'd take care of his mage, no matter what that meant or how uncomfortable it made him.

"What's going on?" he asked, gently squeezing Ansley's shoulders.

Ansley sighed, and Parker felt his shoulders relax under his touch. "I've been working so much," Ansley said. "And don't get me wrong, I love this kind of work. It's like a puzzle, and I'm trying to put everything together, you know? But it also feels like I'm not doing enough, and I don't know how to deal with that. I haven't found any other dragon. We haven't gotten your memories back. What good am I to the others if I can't do this?"

"You're their friend. They care about you more than they care about your spells."

"Maybe so, but they want their dragons, and they deserve to get them back. It's not fair that I'm the only one who has his back."

"If there's one thing I know about you, it's that you won't give up until all of them are here. Your friends know that, too, and I'm sure they're impatient, but they trust you. They know you're doing everything you can, and that's all that matters."

"Maybe. It's kind of terrifying to hold their happiness in my hands. What will happen if I can't find the other dragons?"

It was good to see Ansley wasn't crying anymore and that he was confiding in Parker. Parker hadn't thought that would happen for a long time, and he felt happy that Ansley trusted him enough to have this conversation with him.

"Why don't you have some lunch?" Parker asked, gently guiding Ansley toward the desk.

He peered back at the worktable, trying to understand why there'd been an explosion. Maybe he could do some cleaning up while Ansley ate, although if he was honest, he was kind of afraid to put his hands on that table. The explosion hadn't been big, and Ansley was fine, but it was still too close for Parker to feel comfortable.

"I should eat something," Ansley agreed with a grumble.

He moved toward the table, letting go of Parker, and Parker watched him. He'd known how much he cared about Ansley, of course. He'd been telling himself it was the bond between them, but he'd already decided that even if that was the reason, he didn't care why he felt this way. He just knew he did and that he wanted to do something about it.

But would Ansley want that, too? Maybe it was time to get to the bottom of it and their relationship and find out how Ansley felt. More importantly, it was time to find out what he wanted. They needed to spend some time together, and Parker was ready to provide a distraction so that Ansley could spend a few hours away from his office. They still had to talk about the kiss, and while Parker wasn't eager to do that because he was afraid of rejection, it was all part of a bigger conversation they couldn't avoid anymore.

"I need your help with something," he explained.

Ansley had taken a bite of the sandwich Parker had brought him, and he quickly swallowed. "What is it?"

He looked eager in a way he wouldn't have been a few weeks ago. Maybe he was finally getting used to having Parker around, which was what Parker had been hoping for. "Well, I haven't explored the castle much. I poked around, and I know where most of the main rooms are, but there's more to it, and I'd like to explore it."

Ansley stared for a moment. "Then explore it. No one's going to say anything or try to stop you. This is your home as much as it's ours."

"I'm aware. I was wondering if you wanted to do so with me."

Ansley lowered his sandwich and grimaced. "I wish I could, but you know how much work I have."

"I also know that staying locked up in your office obsessing over it isn't helping. Wouldn't it be better to distract yourself for a few hours? I'm not taking you away from your work for days. It's just to give your brain some time to relax and think about something else. I don't know about you, but when I'm stuck on a problem, it always helps me not to think about it for a while. It's when my brain does its best work."

Thankfully, instead of looking uncompromising, Ansley appeared amused. "Your best work?"

Parker laughed. "You know what I mean. I understand how important your work is and that you don't want to put it aside, especially for something as ridiculous as exploring the castle with me, but I truly believe it would be beneficial for you. You're stuck, whichever way you turn. Maybe try taking a different route?"

Parker expected Ansley to tell him to fuck off, or at the very least, that he didn't have the time to take away from his work and send Parker on his way. Parker could deal with it if that was how Ansley wanted to do things, but he believed every word he'd just said. Ansley needed some time away, and Parker was here to provide that.

"All right," Ansley eventually said.

Parker blinked. "I'm sorry?"

Ansley's smile grew. "I said all right. I'll come with you. You're not wrong when you say that what I'm doing clearly isn't working. Maybe it's time to try something else."

"I'm happy to provide any distraction you might need."

Ansley laughed. He always looked young, but he was almost painfully so when he was like this. It made Parker wonder what Ansley would be like if he didn't carry the weight of the world, or at the very least the weight of his friend's expectations, on his shoulders. He wanted to do right by them and help them, and nothing would stop him from doing just that, but he was too hard on himself in a way even his friends weren't. Maybe it was time for Parker to step up and help him shoulder all the responsibilities he'd placed on himself.

Ansley quickly wolfed down the rest of his sandwich. As soon as he was done, he got to his feet and stretched, and Parker had to look away before he did or said something stupid. Ansley was adorably rumpled and exactly Parker's type. The magic knew what it was doing when it paired them.

"We can go now," Ansley said.

Parker eyed him. "You want to go now because you want to come back as soon as possible."

"You caught me. I agree I need some time away, but you won't be able to keep me back for too long. I hope that whatever we end up doing will help me see what I've been missing, and if I do, I'll have to come back."

Parker sighed. "Fine. Let's go." This was why he'd come, after all.

He didn't really care about exploring the castle, even though he quite enjoyed the place. It was pretty in a way he hadn't expected, and he was still in awe of the fact that this was his home now.

But the only thing he cared about was Ansley and the way he was smiling now that he was leaving his work behind. Exploring the castle would be worth it, even if this was the only result Parker got from his brilliant idea.

It had never been like this with Byron.

Ansley couldn't stop looking at Parker as they walked through the hallways. Parker seemed excited, almost as if Ansley had taken him to visit a famous monument or something, even though they were just walking down the hallway of a castle they called home. Ansley could understand it was incredible to Parker, but it still touched him as something he could never have done with Byron.

For a moment, he tried imagining how things would have gone if Byron had been himself rather than Parker. What would have happened when Ansley found him? He didn't think Byron would have been happy to see him. He might have resisted coming back to the castle with him, and when he'd come, it wouldn't have been willingly. He would have because he'd always seen being Ansley's dragon as his duty, but it didn't mean he'd been happy about it. He wouldn't have taken Ansley on a tour of the castle that Ansley didn't need, and he certainly wouldn't have brought him lunch. He wouldn't make Ansley smile as much as Parker was, and he would have kept his distance unless there was something Ansley needed his magic and his dragon form.

But Parker was nothing like that. He was wonderful, and Ansley had never been as much in love with Byron as he was with Parker. Maybe he felt like this because he knew Parker was available this time, or maybe it was just because, as Parker, he was a better man than Byron ever had been. Whatever the reason, it didn't matter. The only thing that did was how Ansley felt, and after what Matthias had told him, he wondered.

Did he really have a chance with Parker? Because if he did, he wanted to take it and never let go. He wanted to surrender because if Parker wanted him, it meant they could be happy together.

"This place is incredible," Parker was saying, peering out a window. "I mean, from the outside, it's beautiful, but it's the inside that really does it for me. It feels like a home, not just a castle, you know?"

"Well, we've been living here for a long time." Ansley hesitated. "I just wanted to tell you that I'll do everything I can to get your memories back."

Parker turned to face Ansley. "What brought this on?"

"I can only imagine how awful not remembering anything is for you."

"Well, it's not the easiest thing to deal with, but I made my peace with it a while ago. Honestly, I don't need you to promise anything. I don't need my memories back. It would help when it comes to protecting you, but from what I know about Byron, he was a dick, and I don't want to be that to you."

"You never could be."

"I hope not." Ansley's mouth was dry. They still weren't talking about what was on his mind, but it was a step forward. "If you don't want the memories back, then what can I do for you?"

"You've already been doing enough."

"You need help."

"I can deal with this on my own" Parker took a step forward. "I want *some* of my memories back, but only to keep you safe. I couldn't care less about Byron and what he thought of you because it has nothing to do with what *I* think of you or how I feel."

Ansley's heart stuttered. "How you feel?" His voice was little more than a croak, and he quickly cleared his throat. He couldn't mess this up. He needed it to go well, and just maybe, by the time the conversation was over, he and Parker would be one step closer to being together.

That was all Ansley wanted. He'd made his peace with the fact that he'd never have Byron, but he didn't need Byron. He had Parker now, and the memories of Byron were fading. It was easy to forget about him when he hadn't been anything like Parker. Even though they looked the same, the memories of Byron's behavior and what he'd said to Ansley were getting easier to ignore because Ansley knew that Parker would never do anything to hurt him.

Ansley stayed where he was, holding his breath as Parker took yet another step forward. They were by the window, and Ansley could feel the cold of the stone radiating from it. It helped keep him cool, which wasn't easy, considering how flustered he was.

Things didn't get better when Parker reached for him. It was far from the first time they touched, even after Parker had become Parker. Just a few minutes earlier, Parker had hugged Ansley, and it had felt so damn good. For the first time since he could remember, Ansley had felt safe and protected. It didn't matter that Parker didn't remember how to fight. When it was important, he knew what he was doing.

"I want you, and I'm done resisting," Parker murmured, cupping Ansley's cheek with one hand. "I don't know if it's because of the bond, and frankly, I don't care. Even if it is, it doesn't mean that what I feel for you isn't real. It feels very, very real, and I hope you feel the same way."

Ansley tried to swallow, but it was hard. "I don't know if it's the same way, but I'm in love with you," he whispered, terrified of how Parker would react.

Parker smiled. "Good, because I'm in love with you, too."

Ansley's heart pretty much exploded. He sucked in a breath, knowing he needed to say something but having no idea where to start. Once again, Parker took charge. He kissed Ansley, almost as if he didn't need Ansley to explain how he felt. Maybe he didn't. Words weren't always needed when it came to emotions.

Ansley pressed forward and wrapped his arms around Parker's waist. His entire body vibrated, but for once, his mind finally quieted down.

He was home. He was back where he'd always belonged, and if he had any say about it, he was never leaving again. His place was in Parker's arms, and as long as Parker wanted him, that was where Ansley would be.

"What do you want?" Parker asked, his lips hovering close to Ansley's.

They'd shared their first kiss, but Ansley wanted the second one, then the third, fourth, and so on. He wanted Parker to kiss him forever. Would it be too much to ask? "Anything you're willing to give me."

"Well, I'm willing to give you everything. But I realize that with things being so complicated before, you need space."

"I don't need space." Ansley clung harder to Parker. "I only need you. I don't care how I felt before or what happened in the past. You're a different person, quite literally, and it's been so long that I can forget about Byron. I only want you, and I want you in a way I never wanted him. I don't care about before, just about what we can have now and in the future. It's time to let go of the past for both of us."

Because Ansley wasn't the only one who still suffered because of what had happened back then. Parker was, too, and Ansley wanted it to stop. Parker deserved to be happy as much as Ansley, and it was time for both of them to let go of Byron.

Parker smiled. "Let go of the past?"

Ansley grinned. "Exactly, and focus on having a future together."

When Parker leaned forward, Ansley kept the kiss gentle and sweet. Parker was clearly confused, but he didn't stay that way for long. When Ansley turned around and grabbed his hand to pull him down the hallway, Parker laughed and easily followed him.

He trusted Ansley, and Ansley trusted him. He wouldn't have felt this way with Byron, but this was the last time he thought of the dragon that way. There was no Byron anymore. There was only Parker, and Ansley was ready to start their future together on the right foot.

By getting Parker into his bed.

Ansley laughed when Parker stumbled and almost fell on his face as he climbed the stairs. Parker tried to grab him, his heart racing and a smile on his face, but Ansley danced out of the way, and Parker could only watch him go.

He couldn't remember ever having so much fun with a one-night stand. He didn't think he had, but he'd been afraid of letting most people close. He couldn't afford for anyone to discover his secret, and having a lover would have been too dangerous. But he didn't have to hide from Ansley. Ansley knew everything, and he wasn't afraid of Parker. He wanted him, and it wasn't something Parker was used to, but he was ready for it.

So, so ready.

They rushed through the hallways, making their way to Ansley's rooms. The room Parker had been staying in didn't feel like his yet, and he wanted to be comfortable. Besides, Ansley hadn't asked him where to go. He ran ahead, clearly as impatient as Parker to finally fall into bed together. They'd both been resisting, but that was over now.

Parker was a bit wary about what would happen after he'd found that passage in the book. He had a hard time believing that mages and dragons could exchange magic and bolster each other. It felt like something Ansley would know if that was the case, so maybe the book was wrong, but what if it wasn't? What if, since Ansley and Parker had never been together like this before, Ansley had no idea this was a thing? Maybe he didn't talk about sex with his friends. They'd lived together for a long time, but it didn't mean they were comfortable talking about that, especially considering what had happened to the dragons. They'd probably avoided this topic because it was too painful.

Ansley slammed open the door that led to his suite of rooms and ran in. Parker was right behind him, slamming the door shut before following him deeper into the suite. He didn't have to ask to know that Ansley was headed toward his bedroom, which was where Parker wanted to go.

He was right behind Ansley, yet when he stepped into the room, Ansley was already half-naked. He threw his t-shirt at Parker's head. Parker tried to catch it, but it hit him in the face. He pulled it off, and by the time he did, Ansley was pushing his jeans down his hips.

Parker stared. Ansley was even better than he'd imagined, and he'd done that a lot. Ansley didn't seem to have any trouble getting naked, and his underwear followed his jeans, dropping to the floor, leaving Ansley fully naked for Parker to stare at.

Parker wanted to lick him all over. He wanted to do so many things to Ansley that he didn't know where to start, especially since this was their first time together. He hoped they'd have many more, but there was no guarantee, especially with Carlyle back.

But Parker didn't want to think about Carlyle. The only person he wanted to think about was Ansley, and how could he not? Ansley was offering himself to Parker, looking shy but sure of himself. He knew Parker wanted him, but after finding out that Parker's old version had kept Ansley at arm's length, Parker felt he needed to show the man how much he wanted him.

It would be far from a hardship.

They stared at each other for what felt like an eternity, but Parker wanted more. His dragon was more than okay with that, and it kept pushing until Parker stepped closer. Ansley audibly swallowed and moved back, and Parker's predator instinct took over.

He pounced.

Ansley squeaked and scrambled back, and it only took one little push to have him spread out on his back like a present that was all for Parker. Parker had no patience and wanted nothing more than to be naked with Ansley, so he pushed down his pants. Ansley's eyes widened when he saw Parker wasn't wearing underwear, and Parker grinned. "I don't like feeling constricted."

That seemed to be fine with Ansley. He watched as Parker finished undressing and, as soon as Parker was naked, reached for him. Parker took his hand and allowed him to guide him to the bed, where he wanted to go.

He stretched out on his back and allowed Ansley to take the lead. He looked a bit like a skittish horse, which Parker understood. Byron had never wanted this with Ansley, and if Parker was in Ansley's place, he'd have a hard time believing this was true, too.

Ansley knelt and looked down at Parker, never looking away as he placed himself between his legs. He put his hands on Parker's knees and slowly dragged them up Parker's thighs in a move that was both exquisite and torture.

Ansley skimmed his fingertips up all the way to Parker's cock, but he didn't touch it. Instead, he looked at Parker, and Parker's breath hitched at the depth of emotions he could see there.

"I don't know where to start," Ansley whispered. "I've wanted this for so long, and I didn't think I'd ever get it. It's like a dream, you know?"

"I know. We can do whatever you want, whatever you're ready for." Parker would bow to Ansley's demands, and not only because he wanted to give Ansley everything he'd ever dreamed of. He wanted what Ansley wanted, and he didn't understand why Byron hadn't.

Byron had been an idiot.

Ansley leaned down and kissed Parker. Parker made a pleased sound and buried his fingers into Ansley's messy hair, intent on making it even messier. He finally got to touch Ansley, something he'd imagined many times, and now, he got to do it.

He skimmed his fingers along Ansley's collarbone, hoping not to spook him. Ansley smiled, soft and warm, telling Parker his touch was welcome. Their next kiss was gentle, but Parker could feel the passion in it. This wouldn't be just sex for either of them. It never could be. They should talk about it and what it meant, but not now.

Parker opened his mouth to Ansley. It felt good not to have to make decisions after everything he'd been through recently. He trusted Ansley not to hurt him. He hadn't until now, even when it would have been easy for him to.

Ansley looked good when he was in control. He kissed Parker as if he'd been born to do it, but the rest of him wasn't idle. He gently grabbed Parker's balls and rolled them as he explored Parker's mouth with his tongue. Parker opened his legs to give Ansley better access because he needed more. He wasn't sure what Ansley had in mind, but he'd be fine even with a dry hand job at this point.

That wasn't what Ansley wanted, though.

Ansley suddenly leaned back and sideways, leaving Parker gasping. He rustled under his pillow, his cheeks flushed as he avoided looking at Parker. Parker understood why when Ansley took out a bottle of lube. It had been well-used, and from where it had been hidden, Parker could tell Ansley used it regularly.

That was really fucking hot. What Ansley did next was even hotter, though. He slithered down Parker's body, settling between his legs again. Parker watched him open the lube and slick his fingers, but instead of reaching between Parker's legs like Parker expected, he reached behind his back.

He was getting himself ready for Parker's cock.

That wasn't the only thing he did. Parker's mouth went dry when Ansley leaned over him again and wrapped his lips around his cock. He sucked, then swallowed, driving Parker nuts as he got himself ready for more. Parker wanted to help, but it felt good to have someone take care of him, and he suspected Ansley liked having this kind of control over him. He'd said he'd wanted Parker for a long time and that he was afraid to lose him now that he had him. Parker didn't know how to make him see that he wasn't going anywhere, and he doubted this would be enough, but right now, it was the only thing he could give him.

Parker blinked when Ansley leaned back. He reached for him, wanting to pull him close again, but Ansley was ready for more. Parker sucked in a breath when he realized what was finally about to happen. Doubts and memories of the book slipped in again, but he wouldn't stop this. He wanted to see if the book was right and if the union between him and Ansley would change anything in either of them. Maybe that was what the mages needed in order to be able to defeat Carlyle permanently.

Parker watched as Ansley scrambled on top of him. His fingers glistened with lube, and he quickly cleaned them on the sheet, making Parker snicker. Ansley's cheeks went even redder, but he didn't stop moving, not even when Parker grabbed his hips.

Ansley reached behind himself and held Parker's cock up. He held his gaze as he placed himself into the right position, then slowly sank onto it. His body was tight and warm. It welcomed Parker, and the knowledge that Parker belonged here, in Ansley's arms and in his body, filled Parker. This was right.

It was what they needed to do, and Byron had been wrong to keep Ansley away.

Parker wouldn't make the same mistake.

Ansley was beautiful, even though he didn't believe it. He stared down at Parker as he moved, his eyes wide, his cheeks flushed, his lips parted as if he were about to murmur Parker's name. Parker wanted to roll them until Ansley was under him, to fuck into him until they both came, but not this time.

Ansley rocked against Parker, his back arched, his hands flat on Parker's chest. His cock was hard, and Parker grabbed it, needing Ansley to come soon. He pressed his thumb against the slit, grinning when Ansley's ass tightened around him.

Parker hooked a hand behind Ansley's neck and pulled him down to kiss him. Something built inside of him, and not just his orgasm, although that was close, too. No, this was something Parker had never given much thought, but that had always been inside of him. He hadn't known it was his shifter magic until Ansley had explained it to him, but he did now, and he wasn't surprised by the fact that it was reaching for Ansley.

Ansley had said that while he could manipulate and use magic, he didn't have magic of his own. Parker did because he was a shifter, and that magic wanted Ansley. Something shifted deep in Parker's core, and he could have sworn Ansley started glowing. Parker's dragon roared along with Parker, who bucked his hips up and filled Ansley as he came.

Ansley shuddered and cried out. Parker's hand was still on Ansley's cock, and he jacked Ansley through his release as well as he could. It wasn't easy because he was distracted.

The light coming from Ansley brightened until it hurt to look at him. Parker screwed his eyes shut and held Ansley, letting whatever was happening wash over them.

By the time everything slowed down again and Ansley slumped on top of Parker, Parker was exhausted but finally at peace. He felt more settled, and he knew they'd done the right thing. He and Ansley belonged together, and the magic had always known that. It had taken them too long to realize the same, but now, they were one, and it wouldn't ever change.

The only thing left to do was to find out what it meant for both of them and for the fight waiting for them.

CHAPTER THIRTEEN

"Go lower," Tyne said with a snarl.

When he tried to hit Parker's legs, Parker danced out of the way. Tyne's eyes widened, but that didn't stop him from pushing forward.

That was what Parker wanted him to do.

Now that Parker and Ansley were together, Parker had an easier time defending his mage. Maybe it was because the bond between them was finally complete, or maybe because they'd stopped trying to keep the other away and accepted that they were in this together. Either way, even though Parker's memories weren't back yet, he felt better than he had in a long time and was ready to take on Tyne.

Tyne walked around Parker, trying to find a weakness. Parker knew he had a lot of them, but Tyne was clearly struggling to find a starting point.

Tyne was bare-chested, which was a sight. Parker was fully invested in his relationship with Ansley, and it wasn't like he wanted Tyne, but he had eyes and couldn't exactly look away. The man was built with broad shoulders that bulged with muscles, clear skin, and tattoos. Parker wanted to ask about them, but he didn't dare. He didn't have to ask about the massive dragon on Tyne's back.

He knew who the dragon was.

Tyne was careful, but one of them needed to move first. Parker waited and grinned when Tyne shifted his weight forward. He knew what was about to happen, and sure enough, Tyne reached for him.

He grabbed Tyne's wrist, then tried to pull him forward to make him lose his balance. The problem was that Tyne had much more training than Parker, and he used that to his advantage. He quickly shifted their grips, and Parker found himself being grabbed. Tyne twisted, raised Parker's arm, then hauled him over his back, and threw him onto the mats. The air whooshed out of Parker's lungs, and he stared at the blue sky, wondering what had happened.

"You're going to have to show me that move," he said.

The mage appeared above Parker. "I will, but good job. What have you been doing? You weren't this good a few days ago."

Parker flushed, thankful he'd already been heated because it meant Tyne couldn't see it was because of his question rather than because of the fight. "I've been practicing."

"Well, continue to practice. We'll get you in fighting form in no time."

Tyne offered Parker his hand, and Parker took it. He allowed the mage to haul him to his feet, and they went back at it.

Even though it was getting easier to fight Tyne than it had been before, Parker was still exhausted by the time the training session was over. He grabbed a towel and sat on one of the benches that lined the wall, drying his face as he breathed in and out.

He felt someone sit next to him and peeked. He was surprised to see Jarvis, but he was especially surprised to see the way Jarvis was staring at him.

"What?" he asked. "Do I have something on my face?"

Jarvis chuckled. "Apart from sweat, no. I've been watching you and Tyne for a while now."

Parker grimaced. "So you can see how bad I still am."

"What I can see is how good you've gotten. When you move, it's almost as if your body remembers what to do. It's not perfect yet, but then, you don't have your memories. Or do you?"

Parker frowned. "Is that what you think? I wouldn't have kept it from you and the others if I'd gotten my memories back. No, I'm still very much Parker."

Jarvis nodded, but he was still staring. "Have you been doing anything different, then?"

"What is it with you guys asking me about that? Tyne asked, too."

"It's because we're curious. We didn't expect something like this to happen."

Parker was going to have to tell him, wasn't he? "I did do something different."

"Do you think you could give me details?"

"Not unless you want to find out more about Ansley's sex life."

Jarvis grimaced. "Not particularly. You think it was that? I'm not sure why sex would have changed anything about your memories."

"I don't think it's the memories. I think that the bond Ansley and Byron shared wasn't complete. I've been reading a lot, and I found a book where this guy talks about the bond between mage and dragon. He's convinced the bond can't fully be complete unless they're together and have sex."

Jarvis hummed. "I suppose it makes sense."

"Does it?"

"Well, the magic chooses mage and dragon. I don't know how it happens, but we work together as if we were made for it. Dragons are supposed to dedicate their entire lives protecting their mage, and that would be easier if they had feelings for each other, wouldn't it?"

"So you think the bond makes us fall in love with each other?"

"No. Byron would have fallen in love with Ansley if that

was true."

"You don't think he was in love with him?"

"I know he wasn't. Ansley did, too, which was why he never pushed for anything between them. You're saying your bond wasn't complete because of that?"

Parker shrugged. "I don't know. It certainly feels different now. I mean, before, I wouldn't have known we were somehow linked if I hadn't been told that I was chosen as his dragon. Now I can actually feel it here." Parker touched his chest. "It's like a warm presence. It's almost like I'm finally complete, even though I wasn't incomplete before Ansley came into my life, you know? But I felt something the first time we were together, almost as if the magic was happy we were finally doing that. I wondered if sex was needed, but I thought that if that was the case, you or one of the others would have told Ansley about it. Especially you, considering how close you and your dragon were."

Jarvis leaned back and tilted his head to look at the sky. "I suppose I never thought about it. When I met Marlow, I fell in love with him almost instantly. He was the most beautiful and sweet man I've ever met, and I couldn't believe he saw the same in me. Our bond was always strong, and we got together as a couple almost from the beginning. I didn't think things would have been different if we hadn't."

Parker supposed that made sense. This was the only bond Jarvis ever had. He wouldn't have known to tell Ansley about finishing the bond, and Parker was actually happy about that. It might make him a selfish asshole, but he was glad Ansley had been with him as Parker and not as Byron. Byron wouldn't have taken care of Ansley the way Parker would. He might have been a good protector, but he'd only protected Ansley's body. Parker had every intention of protecting his heart, too.

"I'm glad you managed to make things work," Jarvis said.

"You deserve to be happy."

"I'd be happier if we knew what's happening with Carlyle, but we're making things work."

"We'd all be happier if we knew what's happening with Carlyle. I think we need to have a meeting about this, though."

Parker frowned. "About what?"

"The fact that you and Ansley are together and the way your bond changed because of that."

"I'm not talking about my sex life in front of everyone."

"You don't have to give us details." Jarvis got to his feet. "But this is something we weren't aware of and that we need to know for the future. I can't believe we never talked about it before. Come on. I'll text everyone."

Parker groaned. He'd needed to tell Jarvis about this, but he hadn't realized Jarvis would make it public. Hopefully, Ansley wouldn't try to strangle Parker once he found out what the meeting was about.

Parker wouldn't bet his life on that.

Ansley stared at his phone. He knew why the meeting was being called. Only one thing had changed, and he had no intention of talking about it with anyone, especially not his brothers.

Maybe he could hide in his office. The problem was that everyone would know that was where he was, and they'd come to find him. No, if he was going to hide, he needed to do it in a place where no one would think of looking for him.

Where, then?

A knock on his office door told him it was too late. He groaned and thumped his forehead against his desk, eyeing the window as if he really could get out from there. He might have tried if the door hadn't opened to reveal Penley.

"Do you know what this meeting is about?" he asked, clearly not knowing that Ansley's life was about to go down in flames.

"My sex life."

Penley stopped in front of the desk and looked down at Ansley. "What? Why should we discuss your sex life? I don't want to know what you're up to in your bedroom." He paused. "Wait. How do you *have* a sex life? You're not dating anyone."

Ansley looked up and glared. Penley stared, his expression still lost. Ansley knew when Penley realized what was happening. His eyes widened, and his mouth curled into a small o of surprise.

"You and Parker?" Penley asked, slightly bouncing on the balls of his feet.

Ansley pushed himself out of his chair. "Yes. Me and Parker. Can we not talk about it, though?"

"Why not? I'm happy for you. It was about time the two of you got to this point."

"Maybe so, but I don't think it's worth having a meeting with everyone."

Penley grimaced. "I can't say I disagree. I'm sure there's a reason Jarvis is calling for the meeting, though. Come on. Let's go see what he wants, and if you're lucky, no one will ask what you and Parker are up to in your bedroom."

Ansley groaned again, but he followed Penley out of the office. He knew how everyone would react. They'd be happy for him and puzzled about Jarvis's meeting until Jarvis explained why they were here. There had to be a good reason. Jarvis wouldn't call a meeting to talk about Ansley's sex life, but Ansley had felt something when he and Parker had gotten together. He hadn't known what it was, and he still didn't. He'd put it up to him wanting this for a long time, but maybe there was more to it.

He certainly felt different. Again, it could be because he'd been in love with Parker for a while, but he was more settled, and it felt slightly easier to use magic. It was as if it flowed toward him more naturally, but he'd been telling himself it had nothing to do with Parker and what they'd done. It didn't make sense, and Ansley hadn't been planning on asking any of the mages who'd been in relationships with their dragons if it was normal.

He eyed Penley. As far as he knew, Penley and his dragon hadn't been together that way yet. There would be no asking him how it had felt, but Ansley couldn't imagine asking Jarvis, of all people. He didn't talk to anyone about his sex life, especially not the guy he considered partly like a big brother, partly like a father.

The conference room was already full by the time they reached it. Like Ansley had expected, everyone turned to look at him as if they knew. He glanced at the door, wondering if he could be quick enough to leave, but before he could, an arm wrapped around his shoulders and guided him forward.

"I'm really sorry about this," Parker said.

Ansley sighed. "So you know what the meeting is about?"

"I'm pretty sure I was the one who gave Jarvis the idea of it. I was talking about us."

"That's what I thought. I really don't want to talk about what we do in the bedroom."

"Neither do I, but Jarvis realized something, and I think it's important we hear it."

Ansley was curious now, so he allowed Parker to guide him toward one of the chairs around the table. Parker sat next to him, and Ansley found himself smiling.

When he turned to face the rest of the table, everyone was staring. Penley looked so excited he might explode, and even Tyne's lips were curled into a tiny smile that, for him, was a lot.

Ansley cleared his throat. "Let's get this out of the way. Yes, Parker and I are together."

"We're happy for you," Jarvis said. "And it's the reason we're here."

"I'm not telling you what we do in the bedroom. That's where I draw the line."

"I don't want any details. It's just something Parker said that made me realize we never talked about this as a group."

"Why should we have? We weren't a family before. We became close over the years we worked to stop Carlyle, and even more so since then, but back when we first met, it would have been incredibly awkward to have you tell me about sex with your shield."

Jarvis leaned forward. "Exactly. I didn't think that anything about my bond with Marlow was strange. As you all know, he and I got together almost from the beginning. Our bond was always strong and the only one I knew, but Parker made me realize it wasn't the case for you and Byron."

Ansley took a moment to analyze how he was feeling. The bond had always been between him and Parker, but Jarvis was right. It felt different, like it had deeper roots in Ansley now, like a warm presence in his chest. He'd attributed it to the fact that he was in love with Parker, but could it be something different? "What do you mean?"

"No mage knows a lot about the bond. It's there, but we don't know how it works or how the magic chooses our dragons. I thought that all of you had the same bond with your dragon as I did with Marlow, but I don't think that's the case anymore. Parker found a book that talks about the bond and how to complete it, and he mentioned that the author is adamant it has to be through sex."

Ansley's cheeks flushed, and he looked away. "Well, consider our bond complete."

"But don't you see? We were able to trap Carlyle even

though the bond of some of us *wasn't* complete. If we find all the dragons and complete the bonds, we could be even more powerful than we were back then."

Ansley blinked and turned the words in his mind. "I'm not sure I'm stronger, just different."

"What kind of spell have you tried casting since you and Parker got together?"

"Not many." Mostly, Ansley had been daydreaming. He wasn't proud of it, but he knew how much he'd worked over the past decades, and he felt he deserved at least a week or two to focus on Parker. He hadn't even tried to cast the seeking spell again.

"This is interesting," Keylon said. He'd been taking notes, and the page was already half scribbled on. "What brought this on?"

"I was watching Parker train with Tyne, and I realized he moved differently," Jarvis explained. "It's almost as if being with Ansley woke up the side of the shield bond."

"But no memories?"

They all looked at Parker, who shook his head. "I'm still Parker. Honestly, that's fine with me, although I wish I could remember more about how to keep Ansley safe."

"Well, if it makes it easier for you to act on instinct, it's something at least."

Ansley leaned back in his chair as his brothers continued talking about what the bond had done to Parker and what they could expect. They also shared their experiences, but Ansley was focused on Parker, who was lost in his thoughts.

Ansley knocked their shoulders together. "Everything okay?" he asked in a whisper.

"I'm fine. I'm just sorry I told Jarvis about us."

"I can't say I was happy to find out he wanted to talk about what we did, but I understand why you told him, and besides, it gave me an idea."

"Yeah?"

"I do feel different, maybe like I have a better grasp on my magic. I want to experiment a bit first, but I'm wondering how it'll change casting the seeking spell."

"You're still working on that?"

"I'm not going to stop working on it until I have all the dragons back." And for once, Ansley felt actually hopeful about being able to do so. He wouldn't know until he experimented, but he couldn't wait to start again.

He looked around the table.

As soon as the others were done talking about his sex life, anyway.

CHAPTER FOURTEEN

Parker bounced down the hallway, eager to get to Ansley. He was done for the day, having trained with Tyne and then spent a session with Jarvis to talk about magic. Parker loved those sessions and was surprised at how much he did.

Jarvis had been discussing magic with the other mages for a hundred years. He'd told Parker he wanted a new perspective, and while Parker wasn't a mage, he was still magical. As a dragon, he was even more magical than the mages, which was saying something. Parker was just glad to have someone to talk to about his theories. Ansley would have listened to him, but he was still locked up in his office, working on the seeking spells. He'd promised he'd find the other dragons, and Ansley wasn't the kind of person who didn't keep his promises.

That was why he and Parker had barely seen each other much over the past few days. Since the meeting, Ansley had been locked up in his office. Every so often, Parker could hear a small explosion, and while he was worried, he'd told himself not to run in every time. Ansley was perfectly fine. He knew what he was doing. Besides, he dragged himself out of the office for meals every day. Parker missed him a bit, though, which was why he'd organized the rest of the day so they could spend it together. He was pretty sure he'd have to drag Ansley away, but he was ready to do it if necessary.

His backpack was slung over his shoulder, heavy with a blanket, food, and drinks. He already knew he wouldn't be able to take Ansley away from his office for long, but he didn't need a lot of time. He just wanted them to spend an hour to-gether, eating and talking. Ansley could go back to the office once they were done, but Parker hoped they could spend the rest of the day together.

He turned into the hallway that led to the offices and slowed down. The pictures had been on the walls since he'd arrived, but he'd never given them too much thought. He'd been focused on the castle, on finding out he'd had an entire life he couldn't remember. Now, he could see the pictures were personal.

He drifted alongside them, smiling at the sight of the mages making funny faces at the camera. Well, except Tyne, who looked like he'd been forced to stand with the others to get their pictures taken. That was probably the case, actually.

The look of the pictures slowly shifted. The clothing be-came less modern, and the smiles on the mages' faces became tenser. Parker was going back in time, and he did so until he reached a picture with people he didn't recognize.

He knew the mages had faced Carlyle at the beginning of the century. The pictures dating back all the way then were strange, with clothing he didn't recognize and less natural po-sitions. He was interested in the faces he didn't know, though.

He eventually found a picture in which all the mages and dragons were present. He didn't know who'd taken it, but that wasn't what mattered. What mattered was that he found himself face-to-face with himself.

He recognized his face, of course. It hadn't changed, alt-hough his expression had. Byron looked pissed as he stared at the camera, his back tense, his shoulders square. Ansley was next to him, but there was some distance between them, and Parker didn't like it. From the way Ansley held himself, it was almost as if he was afraid to make Byron angry. They weren't looking at each other, but their relationship was clearly very different from what they shared now.

Parker wouldn't have it any other way. He hadn't gone back to the attic because he didn't care about Byron's things and who he'd been before. Maybe in time, he'd want to go through those things, but for now, he was fine never doing it.

He stepped away from the picture with a shake of his head. He didn't think any of the mages would ever be able to give him his memories back, but that was all right. He didn't want to remember how he'd been back then. He hadn't made Ansley happy, and that was his main goal now. He didn't understand his old self and didn't think he ever would.

The door was closed when Parker reached Ansley's office, and he knew better than to barge in, so he knocked. When he didn't get an answer after knocking a second time, he pushed open the door.

He took a moment to look around the room once he was in. Ansley was at his desk, writing something. He didn't seem to have heard Parker, and Parker wasn't surprised.

He cleared his throat, grinning when Ansley squeaked and looked up at him.

"That's not funny," Ansley said with a scowl. "I could have been writing something important."

"I have no doubt you *are* writing something important. Nothing bad happened, though."

"Did you need anything?"

Parker wasn't offended by Ansley's tone. It always took him a moment to get his mind away from work, and until then, he'd be distracted and maybe a bit dismissive. It was Parker's job to pull him away for a few hours. "I do. I need you to step away from your desk."

"I can't. I've been working on the seeking spell again, and it's about time for me to cast it."

"I realize how eager you are to do so, but surely, you can take a few hours away from your job to be with your dragon?"

Ansley glared. "Not fair. You know what you're doing by

using yourself as a carrot dangling in front of my face."

"I do. Come on. I have a backpack full of food and a blanket, and I've been exploring the area recently. I found a great spot from which we can see the castle but spend time alone." Even though the castle was massive, Parker felt they hadn't had enough of that yet. There was always someone with a question, something Ansley needed to do. Hell, there was always something *Parker* needed to do. Now that his shield instincts were coming back, he was training more than ever to hone them.

Ansley looked down at his piece of paper, then back at Parker. "Fine. I suppose I can take the rest of the day off."

Parker beamed. "The rest of the day? I feel so lucky."

"You won't feel lucky if you continue teasing me." Ansley got up and stretched. "Let's go, then. Show me that spot of yours."

There was a bounce in Parker's steps as he guided Ansley out of the castle and into one of the courtyards. He handed Ansley his backpack with a wink, then quickly shifted, taking care not to hit Ansley as he did so. Thankfully, Ansley was used to this kind of situation. He'd taken a quick step back, and he watched as Parker stretched out his wings and shook his body like a dog might have.

"You should shift more often," Ansley murmured as he ran a hand down Parker's flank. "I can see you miss it."

Parker gave Ansley a toothy grin. He did miss his dragon form, but he had more freedom to shift here than he ever could remember having. He wanted to share this with Ansley, so he lowered himself to the stone so Ansley could climb onto his back.

He did so easily, and Parker waited until he could feel Ansley patting his back before getting to his feet.

Then, they were off.

The wind blew around Parker, and he roared in pleasure.

Ansley laughed, and even though Parker couldn't see him, he could imagine the wide smile on his face and the way his eyes sparkled.

They *really* needed to do this more often.

Parker flew for a bit, eager to show off and stretch his wings. He went up and down, then circled around the castle. By the time he landed, his wings felt pleasantly tired, and he stretched them one last time before folding them against his back and shifting to his human form.

"You had fun?" Ansley asked.

"I did."

"Good. You said you'd feed me."

Parker laughed and grabbed the backpack from Ansley. He opened it, quickly stretched out the blanket, then started taking things out. He and Ansley settled on the blanket, sitting next to each other as they ate while looking down at the castle.

From a distance, it looked like it belonged in a fairytale. Parker's life felt like one, so it was fitting.

"I think I needed this, even though I didn't realize it," Ansley said softly. "Thanks for pushing."

Parker wondered if Byron would have. Probably not, considering what he knew of the guy he'd been before.

Thinking of Byron made him wonder. He knew Ansley had been in love with Byron, and he was kind of jealous, even though he was Byron. Parker didn't want to ask this question, but he felt he needed to. "I know you were in love with Byron," he said softly.

Ansley turned to look at him. "I was."

"I also know you carried a torch for him for all these years."

"It's more that I felt I needed to find him, and I wasn't wrong. I did need to find you."

"But I'm not Byron. I'm Parker, and I'm very different from before."

"You are. I'm not sure what you're saying."

Parker swallowed. "Just that I know you were in love with Byron and that I hope you can have the same feelings for me eventually." Because Parker was in love with Ansley, and he wanted nothing more than for Ansley to be in love with him. It wouldn't be the same if Ansley was in love with Byron, even though Parker had been Byron.

Ansley hadn't realized that Parker was so worried about his feelings for Byron, but he should have. Even though Byron and Parker were technically the same person, they were as far from being the same as two people could be. Byron wouldn't have cared about Ansley's feelings for someone he hadn't seen in a hundred years, but Parker had wondered if Ansley could feel the same about him as he had about Byron.

He couldn't.

There was nothing alike about the way Ansley felt about Parker. He'd been in love with Byron, but it had been unrequited, and he'd known it. Even when he'd had hope that, in time, Byron would stop seeing him like an annoyance and fall for him, deep inside, he'd known it wouldn't happen. Byron had already decided that Ansley was his mage and nothing more, and Ansley had started making his peace with that.

Then Byron had vanished, and Ansley had panicked. He'd lost his shield, his dragon, the person he was in love with, and even though he'd known he had to put those feelings aside, without Byron there, he'd failed. They hadn't grown, but he'd focused on a version of Byron that had never existed. Over the decades, all of Byron's hard edges and his assholery had smoothed out in Ansley's memories. He'd carried a torch for the dragon and had convinced himself that everything would be all right once they found each other again.

He'd been right. Everything was all right, but not the way he'd expected. He'd thought it a disaster when he'd realized

Byron had forgotten him and everything else, but it had been a blessing instead. It had given him Parker, and the love he had for him was nothing compared to what he'd felt for Byron.

It had a lot to do with the kind of person Parker was. He was infinitely patient, gentle, and sweet. He cared about Ansley and wanted to keep him safe because he wanted it, not because he felt he had to since he was Ansley's shield. Ansley felt safer with him than he ever had with Byron, and even though sometimes, he wondered what would happen if Parker ever remembered, he didn't really want to know. He didn't want Parker to change because he loved him just the way he was.

He loved Parker and didn't care who Parker had been before and what he'd done. He'd finally gotten his happily ever after, even though it came with complications no one had expected, but knowing what his life could be like and the kind of love he had, he was ready to fight it out with Carlyle and be the one to win more than ever.

"I can't believe this is real," Parker whispered.

He looked at Ansley like he was precious, which wasn't something Ansley was used to, but he loved it. He surged forward to kiss Parker, who made a squeaking sound Ansley wouldn't have expected from him. It made Ansley laugh as Parker wrapped his arms around him and rolled them until Ansley was under him. He loomed over Ansley, but Ansley didn't feel intimidated or wary. Parker would never hurt him.

They kissed again, and Ansley clung to Parker. He was almost afraid that Parker would vanish and that all of this would reveal itself to be a dream, but Parker was solid in Ansley's arms and on top of him. Ansley pulled him closer, craving his weight and pressing him into the blanket and the grass under it. He needed to know Parker was there and that he wasn't going anywhere.

Ansley hooked his legs around Parker's thighs and pressed their bodies together. He could feel Parker was hard, and while he doubted Parker had intended for this to happen when he'd decided to take him on a picnic and a flight, they were alone and in love. Who would blame them for making love under the sky? Tyne would probably grumble if he ever found out, but that was because grumbling was how he did everything.

It felt like Parker and Ansley were alone in the world as they tried to push as close to each other as they could. Ansley was impatient, but he didn't try to get Parker naked. It was a bit too cold for that, anyway. The air was cool on his heated skin, but he knew how easily it could turn to freezing, and there were bits and pieces of him that he'd rather keep warm.

Parker seemed to agree because when he opened Ansley's jeans, he didn't try to get them off him. He lowered them enough that he could free Ansley's cock, did the same with his, then wrapped his warm hand around them both. Between the sensation of his callused skin on Ansley's cock, the friction between their cocks, and the feeling of him caging Ansley and protecting him, Ansley knew this would be quick, and he didn't even care. He wanted Parker to know how much he wanted him. Maybe it would help him feel better.

Coming on Parker's hand would certainly make Ansley feel better.

He whined when Parker twisted his hand and rubbed his thumb on the head of his cock. It spread their precum, mixing them in a way that made Ansley shiver in pleasure when he thought about it. He and Parker were destined to be one, mage and dragon, protectee and protector, but this made them truly one. They were more than just magic and shield.

They were love.

Ansley moved with Parker, kissing him until he couldn't anymore because he was panting so much. The kisses became them breathing against each other and pressing their lips to-gether every so often, but that was okay.

Parker groaned and shuddered. Ansley clung to him, com-ing only a few seconds after him. It was heaven to feel Parker against him, taking pleasure in being with him. More im-portant was what happened once they were both spent, though.

Byron could have found pleasure with Ansley, but he'd never have done what Parker did after that. He didn't jump up, put his cock away, and leave. Instead, he rolled to the side to grab one of the napkins from his backpack and used it to clean Ansley with gentle movements that made Ansley want to cry. He tucked Ansley's cock back into his jeans and put everything to rights before focusing on himself. Ansley could only stay on his back and watch, and when Parker leaned over to kiss him, he sighed against his dragon's mouth.

He was happy.

"We should probably head back," Parker whispered.

"Do we have to?"

"Well, we could stay here forever, but it might get a bit cold for you, and I think you enjoy running water and electricity too much."

Ansley groaned but sat up. "That I do. I can't tell you how long the months felt when we first got to the castle. Do you know how complicated it was to modernize it? We had to share the same bedroom, for fuck's sake."

Parker laughed. "I can't imagine Tyne living with Penley for any length of time."

"It wasn't easy. I wouldn't have been surprised if Tyne had left."

Parker got to his feet and offered Ansley his hand. Ansley took it and allowed his dragon to pull him to his feet.

"But he stayed," Parker murmured. "Because you're a fam-ily."

"And now, you're part of it."

The smile those simple words brought to Parker's lips almost made Ansley cry. They were a family, and he'd do whatever he had to protect it.

They were silent as they packed up everything and got ready to head home. They could see the castle from their position, and knowing it was so close helped. It was their home and where they belonged.

Parker shifted into his dragon form, and Ansley climbed onto his back after securing the backpack on his shoulders. It felt easy and reminded him of the countless times he'd done this before. None of them had been as easy, but now, Ansley belonged here.

He trusted Parker not to let him fall, and he was right to. They landed in the courtyard only a few minutes later, Parker's movements secure. Ansley slid off his back and waited for him to shift back, then they walked into the castle hand in hand.

And right into chaos.

Etta was in the entrance, standing just outside the living area door. She was staring into the room with wide eyes and a hand pressed against her lips. Sandy, Penley's assistant, was there, too. He was paler than Ansley had ever seen him and clutching Etta's free hand with his own. Matthias hovered close by, looking confused and anxious.

Ansley and Parker looked at each other. They moved as one, pushing past Etta and Sandy and into the living area, where they found the mages gathered around a computer. It was on the coffee table, with Keylon and Dallin sitting on the couch in front of it. Penley was behind it with Tyne, who had one arm wrapped around his shoulders. Jarvis's expression was dire, and he was the only one who looked up when he heard Ansley and Parker.

"What?" Ansley asked when he reached him.

"Carlyle contacted us."

"He *what?*"

"Technology has improved so much since the last time I got to experience it," Carlyle's voice, which Ansley would recognize anywhere, drawled from the computer.

Ansley had been terrified of this moment happening for a long time, but he wasn't facing it alone. Parker was by his side, a hand on the small of his back, supporting him silently. It gave Ansley enough courage to face the monster he'd thought he was free of for so long.

"Hello, Ansley," Carlyle said.

His face filled the screen as if he were leaning too close to the camera, which seemed to be the case. His hair was long and as blond as it had been in the past. His light-blue eyes were hard, even though his tone was pleasant. He'd always been a monster in human clothing, and Ansley doubted that had changed.

"So you made it out," Ansley said. He moved away from Parker to face the screen. He was scared, but having Parker made him stronger and braver.

He and the others had kicked Carlyle's ass once. They could do it again.

"No thanks to you," Carlyle snapped. "You should have killed me, because now that I'm free, I'll make you pay for what you did to me." He smiled. "But I already did, didn't I? How have you been without your dragons? How much did it hurt to lose them? That was a genius idea, if I do say so myself. I wanted to torture the bunch of you, and what better way? Now you're all alone and vulnerable, and it'll be nice and easy to kill you."

"Will it?" Parker asked, stepping closer to Ansley and putting himself in view of the computer.

Exposing himself this way probably wasn't the smartest idea. Parker and the mages hadn't talked about what to do if they ever found themselves in front of Carlyle, but it would have been better to keep Parker's presence with the mages a secret. They could have surprised Carlyle when he attacked, and it would have given them an advantage.

But Parker couldn't stay back and listen to Carlyle taunting Ansley. He'd been trying to hurt him, and it wasn't something Parker could allow.

So he stood next to Ansley, glaring at the screen, and took his first look at Carlyle.

He didn't remember anything about the mage. He only knew that Carlyle had spent the past hundred years locked in a stone, and it showed. He was skinny, almost so much that a hard breeze would break him in two. The skin on his cheeks was stretched thin, his eyes were sunken in, and he glared with the hatred of a thousand suns. His long blond hair was pushed away from his face, hanging limply over his shoulders. His fingers, which were on the table in front of him, looked like claws. The sight of him was horrifying, and not just because of the way he looked.

"Color me surprised," Carlyle eventually drawled.

He was trying to behave as if he didn't care about Parker's presence, but there was a glint of fear in his eyes, and Parker was glad he'd been the one who put it there. "No matter what you did, the mages aren't alone," Parker said.

"I suppose they're not. Many things happened since I was trapped in that stone."

"Both I and the other dragons will do what we have to in order to keep our mages safe. That includes killing you."

"I have no doubt that's the case. I only see one of you, though. Could it be you're the only one they found?"

Parker gritted his teeth. He wasn't about to answer that question, but he didn't need to. Carlyle could tell he was the only one there because if the others were, they'd have stepped forward already.

That was okay. Ansley would find the others, and together, they'd fight Carlyle and his minions.

"What do you want?" Jarvis asked. He sounded weary and tired but stood strong, glaring at the screen.

"I just wanted to say hello and confirm I was back. I'm sure you already knew about it, but it's been a while, and I wanted to see you all. Did you miss me?"

"As much as we'd miss a tick," Tyne snarked.

Carlyle didn't seem offended by his tone. He wiggled his fingers. Instead of being cute and endearing, it was creepy. "I suppose I'll see you soon. It's going to take me a bit to recuperate from my time spent trapped in that stone, but I'll be back." He grinned, showing his teeth. "I already am."

He reached for the computer, and his face disappeared, leaving the screen dark.

For a moment, no one said anything. The tension in the room was high, and Parker had no idea what to do about it. Break it? Should he tell the others that whatever happened next, they'd win?

How could he make such a promise? He wanted to help the mages, and he'd be there for them, but there was nothing he could do. They'd have to be the ones to fight Carlyle, and while Parker would do everything he could to support them, it had to be terrifying to be in their place.

"At least now, we know for sure that he's back," Keylon said.

Penley snorted. "Because we had any doubts before?"

"Not after the wave of magic that night, I guess."

Jarvis cleared his throat and looked around at the other mages and Parker. "I know this is what we've feared for decades. I'm not going to say it's not scary because it is, but the situation is nowhere near what it was the first time we had to face him."

"We had our dragons back then," Tyne snapped.

"He had his dragon in the beginning, too. He was in better shape and hadn't spent a hundred years in a stone starving and unable to do anything. We have an advantage. We might not have our dragons, but we've been practicing magic, and now that we know more about the bonds we share, we can use that to our advantage, too. Again, I'm not saying it'll be easy, but we can do this. We can take him on, fight him, and win."

Jarvis wasn't wrong when he said things had changed. They definitely had, and while Parker didn't remember the past, he liked his present and wanted more of this in the future. Well, not more of Carlyle, but more time spent with Ansley and the other mages. More time with family.

To do that, they'd have to get rid of Carlyle, and Parker was ready.

"We need to find the other shields," Ansley declared. "I've been working on the spell, and I'm ready to cast it. I was thinking of seeking out Marlow, but we can choose someone else."

The other mages looked at each other, each of them shaking their head. "Marlow is fine," Penley said. "Besides, you'll find all of them eventually. We just have to wait a bit longer."

"We also have to gear up for the war," Tyne said. "We have many advantages, but it doesn't mean Carlyle isn't dangerous. While Ansley focuses on finding the other dragons, we'll have to reinforce the wards around the castle and train. This isn't going to be nice, and it's not going to be easy, but I believe we can win."

And in the end, that was all that mattered. They needed to win against Carlyle because if they didn't, they'd die, and that wasn't something Parker was willing to accept.

EPILOGUE

Ansley stared at the map in front of him and sucked in a breath, then another. He was terrified, but he'd done this once already, and he'd have to do it another five times. He might as well get it out of the way and see if strengthening his bond with Parker would help.

He really hoped so because they needed more dragons.

He was alone with Parker in his workroom and wouldn't want things any different. He didn't need anyone else watching him if he failed, even though he hoped he wasn't about to do just that. He had the spell, Parker's boost, and a whole bunch of failed spells he knew not to use as an example. The spell had worked once. He just needed it to work another five times.

Unfortunately, Ansley's life was far from perfect.

His personal life was good. He had Parker and his brothers, and they'd always be there for each other. Carlyle was back, though, and everyone had been freaking out. Tyne paced the castle day and night, growling at people and snapping at them to get to work. Jarvis had disappeared into his office, where he was no doubt working on protecting the castle and the people who lived in it.

Ansley's job was to find the other dragons, and he was ready to do just that.

He pushed the fear away, closed his eyes, and tried to calm his racing heart. Parker was completely silent. He wouldn't bother Ansley, which was a good thing, but it made Ansley nervous to have someone watching him so attentively. Parker

200

wouldn't say anything if the spell failed, though. He was there to support Ansley, and he'd do so perfectly.

Because that was how Parker was. He was perfect, so much more so than Byron could ever have been. He gave Ansley a self-esteem boost he sorely needed, and he felt more secure as he finally got ready to cast the seeking spell again.

The herbs were burning in the fireplace, and the candles were lit. Ansley could feel the magic around him, vibrating and waiting for him to order it to do what it needed to do.

He did. He thought of Marlow, of Jarvis waiting for him, of them together. They'd always been relationship models for Ansley and the other mages, and that hadn't changed. Marlow had lost his memory, or at least, that was what they all believed, but it didn't mean he wouldn't remember Jarvis. They were fated to be in love, and everyone wanted to believe that everything would go back to normal as soon as he saw Jarvis again. Ansley realized it was probably foolish to believe that, but he needed it to be reality.

He needed Jarvis to be okay.

But even if Marlow couldn't remember anyone, even if it hurt Jarvis, it wouldn't stop Ansley. He wouldn't be facing this alone, either. The other mages, along with Parker, would be there for him. They were a family, first and foremost, and they'd support each other through whatever kind of pain awaited them when they found their dragons.

Ansley pulled the magic toward him and asked it to answer his question. He felt a push through the bond he shared with Parker and gently pulled on the magic Parker was willingly offering, too. He united the two different kinds of magic together, giving them a purpose that made Parker suck in a breath. There was a flash of warmth just in front of Ansley, where the map was located.

Ansley knew he'd succeeded. He was still afraid to look and kept his eyes shut for a moment longer.

Then he couldn't wait anymore, and he slowly opened them.

The burned spot was there, just like it had been for Parker. Ansley would have to cast the seeking spell a few more times with other maps so they could pinpoint where Marlow was, but they'd found him.

He turned to look at Parker. Parker was staring at him with wide eyes, knowing they'd succeeded. "You found him," he said.

"It looks like I did."

Parker stepped forward and grabbed Ansley's shoulder. "You found him. You know it's him. There's no other explanation."

"But we don't know what will happen when we reach him."

"We won't find out until we do. We expect that Marlow lost his memories, just like I did." Parker turned Ansley around so they could face each other. "But you did it. You found the next dragon."

And since Ansley and Parker were the only complete pair, they'd be the ones to go and get him. Well, right along with Jarvis, but Ansley wouldn't have it any other way.

This was only the beginning. After they got Marlow back, Ansley would focus on the other dragons. Then they could turn their attention to Carlyle.

He wouldn't know what hit him.

ABOUT THE AUTHOR

Catherine is the creator of several series, most of them paranormal, including the Whitedell Pride Series and the Gillham Pack Series. While she graduated in translation, she decided to go the writer's way because it was more fun to create her own stories and characters.

She's been living in Italy for more than twenty years, but she's a daughter of the North—Belgium to be precise—and she misses it so much that she's already planning to move back.

She loves pizza—probably too much—her son, her pets, and of course, books. She sneaks some reading time into her schedule every time she has five minutes free from writing, demands from her various pets and son, and lastly, housework.

Connect with her:

lievens.catherine@gmail.com
BookBub: https://www.bookbub.com/authors/catherine-lievens
Website: https://authorcatherinelievens.com/
Facebook: https://www.facebook.com/catherine.lievens.9
Facebook Group: https://www.facebook.com/groups/411788002341528/
Twitter: https://twitter.com/authorCLievens
Newsletter: http://eepurl.com/c-uvKn

www.ingramcontent.com/pod-product-compliance
Lightning Source LLC
Chambersburg PA
CBHW070840120626

46556CB00002B/814